DEVIL IN DISGUISE

Material Girls Prequel Novel

SOPHIA HENRY

Krasivo Creative

You look like an angel
Walk like an angel
Talk like an angel
But I got wise
You're the devil in disguise
~ Elvis Presley

#BeKindLoveHard

CONNECT *with Sophia:*
SophiaHenry.com

PATREON
INSTAGRAM
AMAZON
BOOKBUB

Chapter One

COOKIE

I'VE NEVER BEEN MUCH of a complainer. Not even when the greasy odor from the fried chicken restaurant next door wafts in through the windows and almost makes me choke. Anger and embarrassment fester under the surface, and some days I wish we lived next to the cinnamon bun factory off Tryon instead, but I never let it show.

But tonight, I'm unusually annoyed by the bright red lipstick Mama swipes across my lips that smells like melted plastic and tastes like wax.

"Quit pursing your lips," Mama commands in her thick Southern accent. "You're gonna get wrinkles around your mouth."

"Like those?" I ask, pointing at her.

"I got those after I had you, smart ass." She scowls. "You should have seen me back in the day," she boasts, her demeanor flipping like a light switch.

Like the narcissist she is, Mama likes to wax poetic about her past, reminiscing as if it's a good thing.

Any other daughter would be sympathetic. Hell, I *should* have some sympathy for her. But I'd have to chip away through too many years of resentment to uncover any.

"I know, Mama. I hear people talking about how you were back in the day all the time," I say, hoping it comes across as a compliment, though she must hear the sarcastic tone.

"This one tonight is a good one, Katrina," she says, moving away to inspect my lips. "Don't fuck it, ya hear?"

Mama's never been mushy. Oh no, Mama has balls of steel and is very cutthroat when it comes to getting things done, including setting me up with cigar smelling, rich old men.

She grabs a glass bottle from the counter and sprays me with an overbearing lavender scent. There's no point saying anything, so, I steel my already frayed nerves and let her finish up.

She squints at me, scrutinizing my face as though she wishes she could change it, then resumes her task of painting my lips. I guess she wants to make sure every inch gets covered with the disgusting—possibly radioactive—lipstick.

"No one is going to kiss me with this nasty shit on my lips, Mama." I retort, looking at myself in the mirror as she continues to fuss over me. "Can't you smell it?"

The shade on my lips is slightly darker than the cherry-red dress clinging to every curve, so tight, it looks like it's been painted on. It's a 'new' dress from the thrift store, but the same old drugstore lipstick.

Mama steps back, scowling as she stares at me.

"By all means, Katrina. You run to the store and grab us a good smelling lipstick with all the money you have in your bank account," she says with a flat look on her face.

I press my lips together, cringing as I remember the reason why I have to do this in the first place: keeping a roof over our heads—even if the roof is a piece of shit apartment in the worst part of town.

By 'apartment,' I mean the one room that my mother and I share in a run-down building with almost sixty identical apartments.

Neither Mama nor I cook so the lack of a working stove for the last five years doesn't matter much. The bathroom is barely larger than a telephone booth, but it works for us.

'Works' is a bit of an ironic word, since the shower hasn't functioned properly and we can only take baths. Most people might be annoyed by the constant drip of the faucet, but not me. That's been

2

my personal lullaby since I was a kid. Maintenance has never been able to fix it—which says everything you need to know about our maintenance people. But, at this point, I might have sleeping problems if they did.

The squeaky ceiling fan is a constant reminder of how much I want to be rid of such an undesirable existence.

In twenty years, when I'm telling my kids about the sounds of my childhood, I swear the sound of that fan and faucet are the two things I'll remember. If only I could remember the voice of my father the same way—but life doesn't always work out the way we plan it.

I would have to have *had* a father to remember his voice.

"What makes this one so special, Mama?" I ask, changing the subject. "How is he different than the rest?"

Mama crosses her arms and shakes her head like she's exasperated with a little child. Ever since she got sick, the revolving door of men she brought home came to a screeching halt, and I had to pick up the slack.

Other girls get amazing birthday cakes and special treats on their sixteenth birthday—maybe even an over-the-top Sweet Sixteen party.

But not me.

Instead of parties and treats, Mama decided pimping me out to rich old men was the best way to kick start my sixteenth year on the planet.

Then again, we had to sustain ourselves. And using men for money is all she's ever known.

Ever since I can remember, my dream has been to go to college, get a degree, and get a good enough job to take myself out of the slums of Charlotte, North Carolina. Several years later and the dream remains unwavering, but sometimes I can't help but wonder if it will ever happen.

"It's highly unlikely that either of you will amount to anything," I remember Mrs. Hodge saying during Biology class a few years ago.

It's funny how, despite years of mostly straight A's and breezing through my schoolwork, one negative comment can stick out in my head above any of my accomplishments.

The comment hadn't been directed at just me. No, she included

3

Andre, my black best friend, too. Though it hurt, it was downright offensive to hear her say that about Dre, because school didn't come as easy for him. He worked hard for every B.

But that was life at our high school. Instead of the awesome dude from the *Lean on Me* movie, we got shitty teachers who didn't care. They were people who could never get a job teaching anywhere else, just filling an open job position because no talented instructors wanted to be at our school.

Most people at school know I'm the quiet girl that loves sitting at the edge of the classroom, taking it all in, but ready to bolt at any second. But I doubt they realize I turn into a 'mistress of the night' after-hours.

How will you ever amount to anything when you've always been nothing?

The thought crosses my mind as I stare at Mama's retreating figure. For a moment, I thought she was the one saying those words, but after paying closer attention it turns out she's been coughing for the past couple of seconds.

All the enthusiasm I mustered washes down my spine like an ice-cold waterfall.

"Are you okay, Mama?" I ask, running toward her, my heart pounding in my chest as she begins to hack. "Don't die on me now," I mutter under my breath.

She's still doubled over when I reach her, but she shoos me away gently and straightens up slowly. "I'm fine, Katrina," she says, her cough subsiding.

I try to smile but my lips fail to move. Despite my anger, Mama is the only family I've got.

"Stop fussing over me and get going already," she says sharply, like she didn't just sound like her lungs would fall out a second ago. "You're gonna miss the bus."

"Alright, alright. I'm going," I say, dropping onto the couch so I can put on my scuffed heels.

Within two minutes, I have the door shut behind me.

I always thought mothers are supposed to make sure that their children have a better life than they had. But that hasn't been my experience. Maybe she really does want the best for me, and prostituting me out to rich men is her misguided way of setting me up for the future.

"Someday, I will have a successful job, make a lot of money, and get out of this shithole," I whisper to myself as I adjust my dress.

Self-consciousness takes over as I shuffle down the hallway toward the stairwell. Waiting for a bus in the skin-tight, cherry-red dress that clings to every curve in a neighborhood like ours is like having a bullseye on my back.

People tend to stare at me whenever Mama dresses me outrageously for certain kind of clients, but I never let them see the swirling emotions. Once I step out for work, I become someone else; cold, calculating, and set on completing the task at hand.

Sometimes, I pray silently that this second persona doesn't become permanent. At the same time, it's been extremely effective in getting me through tough times and pushing me toward my goals.

"Hey Kat!" Dre calls.

I haven't seen him yet, but I'd recognize my best friend's voice anywhere.

"What's up, Dre?" I reply, shivering lightly though it's probably still eighty-something degrees out.

"I'm good. Your mama put you on duty tonight?" he asks.

"Rent's coming up," I reply like he's asking about the weather.

Dre knows everything about my life, not just because we grew up together, but because he's the only friend I have, and he's always been there for me, especially during some of the darkest moments.

His mom is joyful and loving—the mother I never had. Despite having four of her own kids to feed on her meager salary from Kmart, she kept me fed during times my own mother hadn't.

Despite seeing me at every phase of life, and knowing what Mama makes me do, sometimes I think Dre wants more than just friendship. Maybe he thinks he can save me.

Too bad he can't afford me.

Any other eighteen-year-old girl in our neighborhood would be ecstatic at the idea of having Dre interested in them. In fact, some of them have threatened to kick my ass just because they want the attention he gives me.

I'm not completely immune to his good looks and charm—with his curly black hair, gorgeous smile, and lanky, baseball-player's build. He actually resembles the guy who plays Willis in Different Strokes.

But I'm the Arnold to Dre's Willis—meaning, I'm shorter, plumper, and—we're like siblings. I don't have any romantic feelings for him. And he doesn't have the guy who plays Willis' bank account.

If he can't get me ahead, I have no time for him because I'm not the average eighteen-year-old girl in the neighborhood. As far as I know, I'm the only one who has to snuggle up with old, ass men, do whatever they command, and still come home and maintain an almost-perfect grade point average.

A boyfriend is the least of my concerns when I have the weight of keeping a roof over my head on my shoulders.

Getting into North Carolina University is number one on my list of ambitions, and I need a lot of money to achieve that by Fall.

"You need me to wait with you at the bus stop?" he asks with concern. Our gazes meet briefly before I glance away. I appreciate his concern—I always have.

I shake my head. "I'm cool."

His friendship is a relief. He doesn't judge me even though everyone else who knows about my family's situation treats us like outcasts. It's funny, because I know a lot of people in our building are doing illegal things like selling drugs or committing robbery, but I'm not treating them like they're dog shit on the bottom of a shoe.

The opinions of sheep don't matter. We all do what we have to do to get by.

"See you in class then?"

"Definitely," I say, bumping his shoulder with my mine. Before I leave, I pause. "Are you good?" I ask.

Dre has a thing for always bottling up his emotions because he feels like that's how a 'real' man should behave, but sometimes I can get the issue out of him. I haven't been a great friend recently.

"As good as any of us in living this shithole ever are, Kat," he replies with a soft laugh.

"Word," I agree, before patting his shoulder and heading to the bus stop.

Don't fuck this one up, Katrina, Mama's voice rings in my ear as I wait on the bus to South Blvd.

As if anything I do could fuck up our life any more than it already is.

Chapter Two

HARRIS

"HEY, kid! You coming out with us tonight," Colt Jarrett asks, clapping me on the shoulder as I'm loading tools into the bed of my pick-up truck.

I should've seen his visit coming, since I could hear the gravel crunching under his heavy footsteps. He's easily the loudest person on the job site, and it's Friday afternoon.

Every Friday at quittin' time, he asks most of the crew if they're going out with 'the boys' after work. We've been working on the newest building for Commons Property Development, my granddaddy's company—now run by my father—in downtown Charlotte for the last few weeks.

"No can do, Old Man," I reply, keeping a straight face because he's only twenty-six.

"Oh, come on! You're the youngest guy on the site. You shouldn't be the lamest," he says, as if insulting me will convince me, but I don't plan on giving in.

"I'm not even old enough to drink. Going out and watching you dickweeds get shit-faced isn't my idea of a rockin' Friday night."

My age isn't really the reason. Slide someone a twenty or two, and I can get any*thing* I want any*where* I want.

An eighteen-year-old used to be able to buy beer in North Carolina, but over the last few years, they've changed the drinking age a few times. It was nineteen until last year when they raised it to twenty-one. It's like they knew I was approaching legal age and kept dangling the carrot and taking it away.

The truth is, I already have plans tonight. My brother Beau, just got back from a two-week vacation in Greece, and I agreed to have a drink with him to welcome him back.

Hanging with the guys on the crew has the possibility of being fun, except I don't have anything in common with them. Half of them are married with kids or old, single men, and the other half are immigrants from Mexico who don't speak English. They're hard workers even if I can't understand a thing they say.

"Nobody at The Park Elevator gives a shit how old you are."

I sigh as I pull up the collar of my T-shirt and wipe my sweaty forehead. Going for drinks is the least of things on my priority list, and I'm not in the mood to succumb to any form of pressure, even if he claims that it strengthens bonds between co-workers. If Colt continues to hound me, I might blow a gasket.

"I'm starving and exhausted. When I get home, the last thing on my mind will be going out," I reply, hoping I sound as tired as I feel. "The only thing I care about is a hot meal and an even hotter shower."

"You work too hard, Harris," he says, sounding disappointed.

"That's not something I expected to hear from you, man."

His comment surprises me as he's one of the hardest working guys on the job. Which is probably why he loves to go out and tie one on every weekend. Let go of the stress.

But attitudes like that are what I hope to change in our company in the future. Construction work is grueling, especially now—during the summer—when the blistering sun and temperatures hovering in the hundreds threaten to melt our bones. But I'm still out there with the guys day in and day out, working as hard as any of them, praying heat stroke doesn't take me down.

"I'm busting your balls." Colt laughs. "Every single guy on this site needs a hot meal and a shower. But we also need to blow off steam and have some fun—you included."

He's right. All the guys—not just me—need time to relax and recuperate over the weekend. And if I join them at the bar, I can get even more insight into what makes them tick. I can figure out what motivates them and what doesn't. And I get to hear the complaints about management and the company.

One of the reasons I'm hesitant to go out with the guys is because I don't want them to know who I am. The more I drink, the more I talk, and that could get awkward.

Last summer, when I started working construction for the family business, I was only seventeen. I wasn't really a member of the team. Everyone treated me like a kid who got in the way. I didn't even get to do much when it came to building. I get it—I had to earn my status. I embraced my role of apprentice and runner. But this summer, things changed, and I need to capitalize on being invited into the inner circle.

It's one of the reasons I begged Daddy to let me take this job under complete anonymity—the guys think my name is Harris Jenkins. I wanted to know exactly what was happening on our job sites. Daddy— and Granddaddy, surprisingly enough—both thought it was a genius idea.

If only the crew knew who I was and what family I'm connected to.

The truth is that they would grovel and beg me to put in a good word for them, but that would defeat the purpose of what I set out to do. The goal is to make a mark for myself without pulling any sort of favors from anyone. I don't plan on letting my ego ruin the opportunity to impress Daddy.

"Hey, earth to Harris." Colt's fingers snapping under my nose jerks me out of my thoughts. Why is he still here? Doesn't he have someone else to bother?

"Don't do that," I say pointedly and thank the heavens my reflexes didn't kick in and punch him square in the face.

"Alright, kid," he replies with his hands up in mock surrender.

"Call me 'kid' again and I swear I'll beat your ass," I warn.

"You're a twig! That would sound more threatening coming from that guy who yells, 'the plane! the plane!' on Fantasy Island." He laughs. "So, are you coming out with us or not?"

I roll my eyes. "All right, all right. You big puppy." I sigh in resignation.

Colt pumps his fist in the air like a basketball player who just hit a three-pointer at the buzzer. Judging by his reaction, you'd think he was the eighteen-year-old and I was the twenty-six-year-old.

"Be at the Park Elevator around nine," he says, walking away from me. "And don't be late," he shouts over his shoulder.

I started at the site about three weeks ago—the Monday after I graduated from Myers Park High School. Working 6 a.m. to 7 p.m. five days a week has me absolutely exhausted when I get home. At the moment, I have zero social life—which is probably why Colt feels sorry for me. He's eight years older than I am and having much more fun. I must be one of the saddest eighteen-year-olds in North Carolina.

No, in America.

A saying I read somewhere suddenly pops into my head. *Success isn't a fan of crowds.*

The goal is clear; show that I am indispensable in the running of the family business. It's not like Granddaddy had the luxury of messing around and hanging out with friends when he was building his empire back in the day.

"Ugh," I groan, suddenly annoyed with myself for succumbing to Colt's invitation.

Loud music and dancing isn't my cup of tea and that's all the Park Elevator has to offer. I *like* the music they play, I'm just not into having to scream over it just to talk with friends.

My idea of relaxing includes some marijuana that I buy from some black kid in the roughest part of Charlotte. I could probably get it from someone at school, but I feel better going straight to the source. I don't trust the assholes selling at Myers Park to give me straight shit. Last month, I heard some people got weed laced with PCP. That kind of surprise is the last thing I need.

Call me old fashioned, but I'm not into drugs like that. I'm not even into snorting coke like my brother and everyone else in the Charlotte social scene now. I'm all about that relaxed vibe. Marijuana does a better job for me than alcohol does; well, except for a luscious, vintage red wine from Daddy's cellar. But I couldn't be caught dead drinking red wine in front of my macho coworkers. I'd be hazed for life.

My mind wanders over a wide range of thoughts as I make my way home. From drinks with the boys to my upcoming fall semester at NCU. I'm not worried about it, I just hate school. Sometimes, I think I could happily work on a construction site for the rest of my life.

But that would never fly in my family. The weight of being the second born male is almost too much to bear. My older brother, Beau has it easy. As first born, he knows his role; The Heir. I'm the one who has to prove myself. I'm the one who has to come up with different ideas just to be noticed.

All this worry is too much. I'll likely lose all my hair before I'm forty due to how much stress I feel at eighteen. It's not easy being a male in the Commons family.

Twenty minutes later, I'm in my bedroom stripping and flipping on the shower. The feeling of hot water flowing down my skin makes me want to crawl into bed and fall asleep, but I made a commitment to Colt and my brother, and breaking my word isn't an option. That was plugged into my head at a very young age. Your word and a handshake are the only things needed to solidify the biggest and best deals.

I pull on a turquoise golf shirt and a pair of khaki slacks before sliding into a short sleeve button down with multi-color geometric patterns. As I descend the stairs of my parents' house, I pop the collar on both shirts. Just in case I have a few too many, I decide to leave my truck behind and hail a taxi instead.

THE CAB DROPS me off in front of Mangione's, a phenomenal little place serving authentic Italian food. Beau would never meet me at someplace like the Park Elevator. He once called it, 'a club for low-class freaks playing suicide music.'

Yeah, Beau's a dick.

But the big dope is waving at me from the tiny bar and grinning widely. As irritating as my brother can be, he's my only one and I love him.

"Hey!" Beau exclaims as I get within hearing range. "It's my baby brother!"

I can't help but grin back at him and hug him fiercely. "Keep it down, Captain," I say, as I release him.

Beau steps back dramatically, with his hands spread apart. "No, welcome home? No, 'How have you been' or 'How was Greece?'"

I forgot to mention, my older brother can be a bit of an attention whore. He just got back from a two-week vacation in Mykonos. Did he really need a vacation after spending a week in London with Daddy the month before? Evidently.

"Oh, come off it," I reply. "Don't rub your trip to paradise in my face when I just got off a thirteen-hour day of back-breaking work."

"You're the one who begged the old man for that job," he replies, picking up his jacket which had been draped over the bar stool next to his, presumably saving the seat for me.

Work is a foreign word to Beau, someone who's never had to earn a paycheck in his life. He gets everything handed to him, which means he's the one being groomed to take over Commons Property Development, the multi-billion-dollar corporation founded by our grandfather, when Daddy retires. All he had to do was graduate from North Carolina University.

And he did—with honors.

I, on the other hand, have always had to work my ass off. Not because I need the money—my parents provide everything I need and more. I asked for the job in the field—on a job site—to prove my value to the business.

I eye the seat with curiosity before sitting down. "Don't tell me we're not eating, dude. You can't bring me here and not let me eat."

My stomach growls as I inhale the luscious aromas of Italy. I'm so hungry I'm about to make like a termite and start gnawing this chair.

"I ate already, but have at it." He slides me a menu. "I had to meet with Waylon and this was the place he chose."

Was.

Hopefully that means they already met up and I can relax instead of plastering on a fake smile to interact with that nasty old man.

"He's already come and gone, right? I can't stomach food if he's here." I peruse the menu I know by heart. Mangione's has been our family's favorite restaurant for years. My parents are close friends with the owners.

"He'll be joining us shortly."

"For fuck's sake, Beau." My stomach drops and I look up at my brother. "It creeps me out that you hang out with Waylon."

He laughs. "Why?"

"He's like, in his fifties? Sixties?" I guess. "Why is he hanging out with twenty-something-year-olds?"

"Better company?" Beau asks, looking at me over the rim of his highball glass. "Because twenty-year-old women are more attractive than fifty-year-old women?"

"Bullshit," I say, closing the menu and setting it down. "Even twenty is too old for that nasty old, cradle-robber."

I'm about to continue my protest, but Beau cuts me short.

"Don't worry about Waylon. I haven't seen you in almost a month," he says, sounding like our grandfather, someone who preaches about putting family first. "The least you can do is ask me all about my wonderful trips."

"Such a prick," I say under my breath.

"I know I'm a prick, Harris, but I'm the only brother you've got, so deal with it."

I can't help but laugh. Despite a healthy amount of sibling rivalry, we've always had a pretty good relationship.

"Well, Captain, since you've admitted to being a prick, it's my brotherly duty to listen to you brag," I reply, anxious to order food before Waylon shows up.

When we were younger, Beau always loved it when I called him 'Captain' because he would be the one to lead the way whenever we had some prank to pull or something delinquent to do. Years later, I don't think the feeling has changed too much.

Sometimes, I wish we were children again and didn't have this thing with inheriting a company creating tension between us. It's not like we were at each other's throats about it; Beau had always been nonchalant when father harped on him taking over the business.

He has a strong personality and a loud mouth. He's never been a fan of people telling him what to do or having things being forced on him. If someone tries to make my brother do something, he instinctively does the opposite.

He can't play that game now that he's working with Daddy. He's gotta sit down, shut up, and learn the Commons way. Sometimes, I feel like the weight of his eventual 'ascension' to the head of Commons Property Development is one of the reasons for my brother's transformation into a total douche bag; like he wants to make father rethink his decision.

"Sometimes, I wish our roles were reversed," he told me one night while we shared a twelve-pack of beer on the roof of the family mansion. Though, I was only fifteen years old at the time, age never stopped good 'ole Southern boys from raiding their parent's fridge and getting drunk in the moonlight.

Sometimes, I do, too. I'd kill to be head of the Property Development company. Instead, I'll keep working my ass off to forge my own way.

Chapter Three

HARRIS

THE HUM of an Italian love song fills the air like the hum of white noise. Something about this place makes me want to live in the moment and not think about my future. Now that I think about it, that's exactly what I need to do; be in the moment and see where the night takes me.

Beau snaps me out of my thoughts by tapping my shoulder and motioning his chin toward the bar. "You getting something?"

"I will if the bartender ever looks my way. What does it take to get a drink around here?" I call to the man whom I've never seen before. My family spends so much money here, the employees usually climb over each other for the opportunity to wait on us.

The new guy's head snaps toward us, peeved at my audacity. One brow arches as he eyes me. I can't tell if he doesn't think I'm old enough or if he doesn't think I can pay for my drink. Probably both.

"Should I call Roberto and Anna?" I ask, mentioning the owners by first name. Sure, anyone could throw out their names, but the Mangione's have been to our house many times. "Or are you going to get me a Pinot Noir?"

The bartender must be struggling to keep his expression neutral because he looks like he's constipated as he grabs a wine bottle from the shelf above him.

"I could buy this entire restaurant if I wanted to," I mutter, the smug rich kid in me rearing. "And the first employee change I would make is fire that dude."

Out of the corner of my eye, I see Beau smirking at me before he bursts out laughing.

"What?" I ask, wondering what has him so amused.

"I'd forgotten how menacing you can be," he says, still laughing.

"Menacing? I'm a lover, not a fighter," I reply. Though it sounds like I'm trying to convince myself more than I'm trying to convince him.

"You've always had a mean streak, little brother," he says, shaking his head but looking more serious than amused. "You were born a dictator. It just takes a lot to bring it out of you."

"Hunger. Hunger brings out the worst in people," I say chalking my rudeness up to a long day without proper sustenance.

"Can I get you anything else, gentlemen?" the bartender asks as he sets a glass of wine in front of me with a scowl on his face.

"Another," I reply, grabbing the glass and draining half of it in one sip. "And the Chicken Alfredo."

The bartender grunts, but turns around to grab the bottle again.

Beau is silent for a while, and I can't help but wonder what's happening in that maze of a mind of his.

The fact remains that I'll never be as good as Beau in our father's eyes. I'll always be the second son, not his shining star of a first son. Beau has always excelled at everything; academics, sports—everything. I, on the other hand, while being more than average, would always be in my older brother's shadow; barely noticeable.

But Beau always saw more in me. He knows I could run the company if given the chance. Hell, sometimes I think he'd hand it over to me—but can't as long as Daddy's alive. And neither of us are wishing for something tragic.

"Look Beau, as much as I appreciate the gesture, you and I both know, I'll never be a leader in that company if Daddy fails to acknowledge me," I say.

"You're such a drama queen." Beau rolls his eyes. "Daddy doesn't treat us *that* differently."

"I don't want to be your understudy. I want to run my own division."

"Work your ass off in Chapel Hill over the next four years and Daddy will let you do anything you want." He pauses for a moment. "Except run it, of course."

"You're such a jack-ass." I scoff and finish off my first glass, pushing it toward the bartender who refills it quickly.

Before I can further vent, all thoughts vanish from my head when a bombshell blonde appears behind Beau. He must notice my hesitation and the direction of my gaze because he turns around, then slides off his seat.

"Well, hel-lo," he says, his voice silky.

When Beau turns on the charm I need someone to gag me with a spoon.

"You must be Naomi's daughter?" he says, taking the woman's petite hand in his.

"Yes, I am," she replies. The lilt of her voice sounds soft and melodious. "Beau, right?"

He nods in assent and claps my shoulder. "And this here is my brother, Harris."

The lady in crimson regards me silently, sizing me up so subtly that one would barely notice—but I do. Underneath the thick layer of makeup, she may be underage or in her early-twenties, it's hard to tell, but she carries herself well.

What the hell is Beau doing with this woman? He's scheduled to marry the mayor's youngest daughter in August.

The answer hits me like a ton of bricks; Waylon.

Perhaps it is the alcohol, but her intoxicating blend of innocence and confidence intrigues me. It makes me wonder if she's hiding anything—other than fear. The goosebumps on her arms are a clear sign she's on edge.

I nod at her, but say nothing. Disappointment flashes across her face, seemingly taken aback by my demeanor; a sign that she's used to having men fawn over her.

I wouldn't blame them. She's drop-dead beautiful with her full lips covered in deep, red lipstick, her flawless porcelain skin, and high cheekbones coupled with wide, doe-eyes and a bodacious curvy bod. I completely understand why any man would want to take her into his bed.

In the moments I've been analyzing her, she and Beau are discussing something in hushed tones. Not that I'm listening. I have no interest in getting involved in case his fiancé ever finds out.

My mind wanders. Maybe she's a stripper. Maybe he's discussing his bachelor party.

Which, should be *my* job as the best man.

Too bad I'd never order him a stripper, and he knows it. I don't want the wrath of LuAnn Whittaker on me.

"Hey Harris." Beau turns, facing me full on. "Keep our guest company, will you? I need to make a call at the phone booth."

I shrug as if I'm unaffected by the lady in red. She seems to be wary of me, so I try to loosen the tension.

"What's your name?" I ask, gesturing for her to take a seat while trying to spark a conversation out of courtesy.

After what could have been ten heartbeats, she finally opens those full red lips.

"Kat," she replies quickly as if my question annoys her.

As a Southern gentleman through and through, I usually have the utmost respect for women. Perhaps it's the booze in my system, or her standoffish attitude, but I feel like teasing this girl.

"A feral nickname," I drawl, "but I presume that's not on your birth certificate. Humor me."

Her eyes focus on mine like she wants to extract my intentions, then she relaxes a little.

"I'm Katrina," she says, sounding tired.

I snap my fingers toward the bartender to signal that I need his attention. "I'll take a water," I say to him as he reaches us. He still doesn't look too happy to be tending to me. "And what will the lovely lady be having?"

"A glass of chardonnay will be just fine," she replies quietly.

"Brimming with both beauty and class," I compliment with a sly grin, then relay her drink request to the bartender in case he missed it. "Katrina. That's a beautiful name."

She lowers her head slightly as if embarrassed by my praise, but the smile on her lips is genuine. I can tell by the way it reaches her eyes. She must feel more comfortable now.

"Are you always this nice?" she asks, looking up at me. Beneath her thick, black eyelashes are hypnotizing grey eyes.

"I'd like to think so," I reply, shaking my head out of the momentary daze, "but my brother just said that I was born a tyrant."

"Well, I can picture you that way, too," she replies. "You look strict —or rigid. And I saw the way you treated the bartender."

Beau walks back to us with another man in tow before I can respond to her observations.

"Katrina, Harris, this is Waylon Harding," Beau introduces us. "He's an acquaintance of mine."

I've seen Waylon Harding before—from afar. He's been in Daddy's circle of associates for years. But honestly, I don't remember him very well. My first impression is that he looks like a bull with long, arms like a crane. He's wearing a thin, long-sleeved shirt, and I can see his biceps bulging through the fabric.

I wonder how the two men started hanging out. Waylon looks more like a private security guard than one of Beau's party-loving fraternity brothers or business executives he entertains on behalf of the company.

"Harris! Look at you!" Waylon exclaims. "I haven't seen you since you were knee-high to a grasshopper!"

The man engulfs my hands in his like a vice and it's taking all my willpower to maintain my poker face. If he's trying to pass a message across, I understand it loud and clear.

Chapter Four

COOKIE

THE SUNLIGHT WARMS my eyelids until I have no other option but to stop ignoring the fact that it's daylight and I need to wake up.

Why does my head hurt so damn badly? And where the hell am I?

I open my eyes to find a strange, large man lying next to me, his tattoo-covered chest rising and falling softly.

That's never happened to me before. I've always been fully aware of who I was going home with. I carry mace in my pocketbook just in case I feel uncomfortable.

I totally would have maced this dude.

He's not one of the men I met last night. I remember them well. Waylon, Beau, and his brother, Harris. After an initial instant attraction, I'd been disappointed to find out Harris wasn't my date. Then again, he's the kind of guy I'd always dreamed about having a real relationship with. Well dressed, dirty-blonde, Brad-Pitt hair, a playful smile, and full of compliments that seemed genuine. Instead, the other two swept me away from Harris quickly and—

Suddenly, bits and pieces of the night flash in my mind. Beau walked me to Waylon's car, but he didn't get in. Waylon and I each drank a glass of champagne before we arrived at an alley off Central Avenue. When I exited the vehicle, my stomach was swirling so much,

I almost vomited on my black patent heels. When I saw the large, tattooed man with small scars slashing his face move toward me, I'd screamed and kicked, thinking he was there to kill me—or at least hurt me.

When the intimidating man spoke, he sounded like that Russian boxer from *Rocky IV*. But he never touched me.

The stranger didn't, but Waylon did.

I remember digging my heels into the gravel and trying to back away when he'd dragged me to the huge man with the Eastern European accent.

I lift my hand to my cheek as the image of Waylon slapping me across the face comes back to my memory.

That's the last thing I remember. With as many men as I've slept with, I didn't expect one more to rattle me this much, but I just can't shake off the weird feeling about how last night went down.

I pull the comforter up, clutching it against my bare chest. I'm naked in bed with a man I don't know in what looks like a lavish hotel based on the surroundings. Ornate gold gilded mirrors, a king-sized bed with luxurious linens.

Suddenly, the sleeping stranger wakes up, his lids fluttering as he stirs. Piercing hazel eyes inspect me reverently as if I'm a sculpture at an art gallery, and it's unnerving. Especially since I have no clue who he is or how I got into bed with him.

After what seems like ages, I finally gather the nerve to break the silence. I squeeze my eyes shut before asking, "Can you tell me what happened last night?"

"I saved your life," he says in a matter of fact, though heavily-accented tone.

"I understand that," I whisper, remembering how Waylon treated me.

"I do not think you do. But we will discuss this another time."

"Did we—" I cast my eyes to the bed, swallowing the words instead of saying them. When did I become the world's lamest prostitute?

"No."

Relief washes over me, but I can't explain why. Fucking random men has literally been my job for the last two years. "So, um, what's your name?" I ask, barely getting the words out loud enough for him to hear me.

"Stanislav," he replies calmly. He shifts his body, turning toward me and propping his head on his hand. The seemingly casual position that puts his rippling muscles and inked skin on display.

Reluctantly, I pry my eyes away. "Good Lord! That sounds like a vampire."

He tilts his head and his eyes narrow in confusion. "A vampire named Stanislav?"

"Isn't that Dracula's name?" I ask coyly.

By his reaction, I can tell I've gotten the name wrong, but I don't have any clue what the famous blood-sucker's real name is, so I'm going with it. It's not like I'm not worried about offending him. I'll be out the door in ten minutes flat.

"He has no name."

"Um, yes, he does," I counter.

"Do you read books?" he asks in a lazy fashion, rolling his shoulders back and stretching his neck.

"Excuse me?" I'm appalled he has the gall to insult my intelligence. The fact that I haven't read Dracula doesn't matter.

"Have you read this book?" he continues.

"Dracula? No. I haven't."

"You should read before stating incorrect information. Then you will know he has no name," he chides me like the teachers at my high school. The urge to prove him wrong kicks in.

"His name is Dracula." I bite my lip, trying to think of the character's first name. "Something Dracula."

"He is Count Dracula. That is all," Stanislav concludes.

"Count Stanislav Dracula," I tease in a really bad fake foreign accent.

The Russian just looks at me with a tired, almost bored, expression. "Are all Americans this way?" he asks.

"What way?"

"Uneducated." The word drips with European disdain.

The war veterans who live around the block used to ply Dre and I with tales of their exploits in Europe and how Europeans think Americans are a bunch of loud, selfish, uncultured swine. Evidently, the veterans weren't telling tall tales; my very own European client is treating me like I'm a second-class citizen, but I don't let my emotions find their way onto my face.

"I think you mean stupid. Are you asking if all Americans are as stupid as I am?" I ask pointedly with an airtight poker face.

The Russian doesn't show any shred of remorse. Perhaps he doesn't feel the need to be apologetic to a prostitute or maybe he was just made that way; blunt.

"You try to make this joke using book you have not read. Then you defend your ignorance. Is very American thing to do."

"If you hate us so much, why are you here?" I ask, pulling the white blanket back across my chest as it threatens to slip off. His penetrating eyes follow the movement of my hand before bringing his gaze to mine. But he doesn't make any move.

"Freedom."

I scan him, trying to figure out what he means. Freedom from what? Communism? I wonder, making sure my face doesn't betray the gears turning in my head. Unable to come up with any possibility besides state execution, I decide I should hear it from the horse's mouth.

"What are you running from?" I ask, cradling my head in my palm as I wait for an answer.

It's all part of the job. Men always love a little pillow talk because what could a lowly prostitute do with any information they divulge. The Russian is no exception.

"I come to America for a lot of reasons, not only freedom," he begins, as I adjust my position on the bed, aware of the fact that I'm still naked under the blanket. "America gives me opportunity to start new life and get out of the mafia in Russia." Stanislav runs his fingers across the tattoos on his body absent-mindedly as if the touch transports him to another place and time.

I lean closer to him, waiting in anticipation for the story to continue.

"My sister, she get trafficked by boyfriend for sex ring."

The statement hits me so hard I feel woozy. It's bad enough my mother coerced me into prostituting to provide for us, but technically, I can stop if I wanted to. We'd be homeless and on the streets, but I still have a choice.

I can't imagine how devastated and hopeless his sister must feel being taken from her family and being forced to have sex with a never-ending barrage of men. At least I know the kind of men Mama's setting me up with. Well, I usually know.

"I get information that she was brought here, to America, and I come to find her."

"I'm sorry," I say, heartbroken for this stranger and his family.

He shrugs. "Sorry does not help," he replies. "Is not your fault."

This makes me smile a little bit. I think I am beginning to like his blunt way of speaking. "How did you end up in the mafia?" I ask.

Somewhere in the recesses of my mind, a voice keeps telling me to wrap up this conversation because Mama is probably wondering when I'm coming home. Not that I care. Let her wait and wonder. The only reason she'd care if I got sold into sex trafficking is because she lost her cash cow.

I'm too immersed in Stan's tale to go back to my own personal hell.

"I get recruited in prison," he says matter-of-factly.

"You've been in prison?" I ask before I can stop myself.

Of course, he has been to jail. He's a fucking Mafioso, I chide myself internally.

His eyes seem so distant, it's obvious that he didn't notice my hesitation. "I murder my mother's boyfriend," he says flatly.

Instinctively, I shrink back, though I don't feel unsafe around him. He notices my movement, but doesn't do anything.

"I go in the apartment while he trying to strangle my mother. It is my instinct," he explains, his voice soothing like he is trying to convince me of something. "My mother, she was prostitute and her new boyfriend always angry with her. Maybe they have fight or he was just drunk, but I cannot control my anger when I see him try to kill her, so I smash vodka bottle on his head and he die," he concludes.

Suddenly, I feel like a horrible person for recoiling when he told me why he was in prison. But after hearing the story, I understand. Some crimes are justified.

"How old were you?" I ask, conscious about the fact that I'm over-reaching now. I don't know how much I can probe before reaching the limits of this man's privacy.

"Sixteen," he answers.

"Sixteen! They put you in prison at sixteen?"

He shrugs. "In my country, kids go to prison for crime like murder. Fourteen—fifteen. I am cold-blooded killer. I get initiated into mafia during my time."

Silence fills the air as I struggle to find the words to say. I'm not used to having this kind of conversation, so I just stay there with my jaw clenching and unclenching like a defendant on trial.

Thankfully, the Russian senses my discomfort, because he changes the topic.

"Anyway, American girl, in the book, Dracula never reveal his name. He is, however, based on Vlad Dracul — Vlad the Impaler."

Back to Dracula. Evidently, he still needs to prove how much smarter he is than I am.

"I knew it!" I snap my fingers, feeling like an actual teenager for a moment.

"You knew nothing," he says, rolling his eyes like Mrs. Hodge did every time Dre or I raised our hands to answer a question.

"Vlad, Stanislav. They sound equally vampiric," I insist in a teasing lilt.

I think he's too annoyed to speak because he just stares at me. Maybe making fun of his name was going a bit too far.

"I can't call you Stanislav," I say, shaking my head.

"I did not ask you to," he says in the flat tone I've come to appreciate.

"Touché," I mutter. But I'm not giving up. "Do you have a nickname?"

"Nickname?" He repeats like the term is foreign to him.

"Like, another name friends call you," I offer.

"My friends call me Slava."

I snort in disbelief. "I can't call you Slava, either."

"Again, I did not ask you to," he repeats, which earns him a smack on the arm and an eye roll from me.

This dude needs to get over himself.

"How about Stan?" I suggest, hoping that will lighten things up a bit. "Stan sounds American."

"After this conversation, I am certain I do not want to sound like American," he says. That condescending European undertone crops up in his words again.

"I'm not stupid, *Stan*," I emphasize the nickname I created for him even though he hasn't approved it yet. "Just because I confused real-life and folklore doesn't mean I'm stupid. It means I'm not a Dracula expert."

"This is obvious," he replies, averting his eyes to the cracks in the ceiling.

"Reading Dracula doesn't make you smart," I protest, turning toward him. He does what he does best—shrugs.

Nothing gets me more fired up than being disregarded as unintelligent. Being a prostitute doesn't automatically mean I'm an airhead. He had a justified reason to kill his mother's boyfriend, I have a justified reason to sell my body for money. Still, the need to prove how smart I am to this foreigner overwhelms me.

"I'm in the top three in my class," I say sullenly, sounding like a spoiled brat.

"I do not know what this means," Stan says, his expression blank.

"Ranking. Schoolwork. *Grades*," I explain. "I have the third-highest GPA in my class."

The blank expression tells me he still doesn't know what I'm talking about, or he's not impressed. Probably both.

"I'm smart," I declare, lowering my eyes and picking at the bedspread, defeated.

"I believe this." Stan nods. "But in the future, you should not use examples of things you know nothing about to make a case. Is easy to discredit you," he says.

When did the Russian become a professor?

"I accept that," I say, agreeing with him. He's right—and it's good advice. It's time to wave the peace offering.

"I didn't mean to offend your country," I say, trying to sound remorseful.

"Is not my country!" He throws his arms up in frustration. "Dracula is Romanian!"

My eyes widen, and I burrow into the covers, fearful he might turn his anger on me. "Sorry!"

"You are frustrating," he declares. Then he reaches out and touches my face. "I will not hurt you, Katrina."

I swallow with relief and close my eyes, enjoying his calloused hand on my cheek for a moment.

"You should be glad I found you. Frustrating would not bode well with the man you were with," Stan continues.

"What does that mean?" I ask, half in shock.

"He would not take you talking back with him. He would smack your smart mouth. Or worse."

"How do you know so much about him?" I ask, emboldened by curiosity.

"I do not know much about *him*. But I know his kind," he replies.

"How do you know his kind?" I ask, willing my breath to settle as panic builds in my blood.

"Because I *am* his kind," Stan says flatly.

His words make me pause. I lick my lips, but my mouth is so dry it barely does anything. "So, my reaction to being frightened every time you raise your hand is justified," I ask, looking for some sort of reassurance.

"Yes," Stan assents to my question.

I feel my heart skip a few beats; I expected reassurance, not agreement.

What I have gotten into?

"If I were going to hit you, I would have already. If I were a man who would hit you, I wouldn't be a man that would save you, would I?" Stan continues, spreading his palms.

"I don't know. You're the one who just told me you were his kind. What did you mean by that?" I ask. He certainly knows how to keep someone hanging on every word.

"We know many of same people."

"Why would you be involved with people like him?" I ask, deciding it's time to dig in and get real.

"Is the business I'm in," Stan replies again, flatly. He's so blunt and reserved, I'm convinced he could lie on every answer and still pass a polygraph test with flying colors. The inability to be ruffled probably comes in handy for someone in the mafia.

Though, I did get him to the point of frustration, so I consider that a win.

"The mafia? Is that what had you hanging around an alley in a shady part of Charlotte at night?" I ask, trying to wrap my head around his words.

"Hanging around? Please explain," Stan asks, his face scrunched in confusion.

"Creeping around? *Walking,*" I emphasize, "in alleys at night?" I offer hoping that he catches on quickly.

"Ah." He shakes his head. "No, that was not mafia business. I will buy that building."

"Why would you want to buy that run-down piece of shit?" The words come out without thinking.

I don't know much about Russia—except that they're the eternal enemy according to American Cold War propaganda—so maybe that building is nicer than the ones he's used to back home.

Or maybe he's going to murder me in that run-down piece of shit.

"I will open tattoo business," he replies matter-of-factly.

"A what?" I ask.

"A place where I tattoo people—a store."

"No, I know what you mean." I wave off his explanation. "Is—is that even legal?" I ask him again, sounding more and more like a kid; which I am.

He shrugs, unaffected by the thought of it being legal or not. The reaction should tell me all I need to know about him. Yet, he's intriguing and exceptionally handsome—if you like tough, tattooed, rugged foreigners. Which, I didn't know I did until now.

"This I do not care. I buy building. What happens inside is no one's business," Stan declares.

"Then how will they know where to go to get a tattoo?" I ask.

"You tell me you are smart." He reaches out to tap my temple. "But you do not speak this way." He continues, "Your mouth will get you into trouble. Your mouth will get you killed."

"Are you threatening me?" I ask him, trying to sound unafraid but preparing to spring off the bed if he tries to grab me.

"Is not me you need to be afraid of, Katrina. Is just friendly warning."

Stan leans closer to me until our lips are inches apart. I catch his scent as I inhale—the faint remains of a woodsy cologne and sweat. Not nasty smelling sweat; manly morning sweat.

"You speak like that to the wrong person and—" He forms a gun with his index finger and thumb and presses it to my forehead.

"I know I have a smart mouth," I admit quietly, pulling my head back from the makeshift gun. I swallow thickly holding back the shock of my new reality and the kind of people I'm involved with now. "I've had to deal with assholes my entire life. I've handled it by growing a thick skin and learning to talk tough."

"Why you deal with assholes?" Stan asks, intrigue lifting an eyebrow. He settles back on the pillow, tucking his arm under his head.

"Mama always had a boyfriend. Sometimes it was for a night, some-times a month. A few guys stuck around for a year or two—until they couldn't handle her anymore." Once I start, memories flood my mind until I can barely see Stan lounging right next to me. "There were even a few nice ones. But they ran away pretty quickly once they realized Mama was only in it for what they could give her, not who they were. It was always the same for as long as I can remember. Until recently."

"How did this change?" he asks.

It's refreshing to have a conversation with someone who's inter-ested in what I have to say and not just humoring me. Normally, my conversations are one-sided. I do the listening while men do the talking.

"Her health and looks deteriorated quickly since finding out she has cancer. She refuses to go to the doctor again because she knows we can't afford treatment," I tell Stan.

I should feel anger or sadness knowing my mother is dying, but the only emotion that surfaces is relief. I know it's selfish of me to think such thoughts, but my mother is the reason my life is so messed up.

Usually, I take responsibility for my actions and not blame others—but in this case—the blame is justified.

"Since she's not able to pull in men anymore, she pushed me into it," I say, steeling my emotions because I can't afford to feel anything or accept sympathy from anyone, especially not the man next to me.

"Where you find these dates? These men?" Stan asks, curiosity reflecting in his tone.

"Where do *you* find dates?" I counter, unnerved by his penetrating stare.

"I don't date. I fuck," he says with so much confidence that it annoys me.

"Aren't you a big, tough man," I reply, rolling my eyes and scoffing.

This Russian probably has a new woman every night to warm his bed, I just happen to be the one on duty tonight. The man looks like he can afford it. If he is staying at this hotel then he definitely can; only the rich sleep in historic hotels like the Dunhill.

I look around the room with its ornate bed, renaissance looking furniture, and view of the city from the window. It seems like there's a Commons' construction crane on every corner, a testament to the recent growth spearheaded by one of the oldest and wealthiest families in the city. It seems like they have a hand in everything—multi-use developments, houses, skyscrapers.

Being part of that kind of family legacy must be nice.

"It's no big deal—it's just sex," Stan says, bringing me back to reality.

At least we can agree on that. It's just sex. No feelings. No attachment. Just a way to earn money.

"You have been hurt, yes?"

"You're pretty naïve for someone who looks like you do." I scan him again and swallow hard. Tattoos creep out of every space not covered by his grimy, formerly-white T-shirt. Though his English is good, his accent is so heavy I can barely understand a word coming from his mouth.

"I don't understand this word. What is 'naïve?'"

"Clueless?" I offer. Though his coal-black eyes burn with fire, his expression is blank. I don't know how to speak a word of Russian, so I can't even try to help him understand in his language. Frustrated, I tap my head and spit out, "Stupid! Dumb!"

I flinch, expecting anger or violence, but he doesn't come at me. He just laughs deep and loud.

"Your mother find you these men." It's a statement, not a question.

I nod. There is no point in trying to cover up Mama's actions; the world isn't all Rainbow Bright and My Little Ponies.

Where had that comparison come from? My longing for a more innocent time?

"Your mother makes you have sex with them for money?" he asks.

"Not just money," I correct him. "Gifts, rent, food. Whatever."

Women are products to be bought and sold. My mother first, and now me. Sometimes I wonder if her mother was the same way. I was hoping to break the cycle by going to college, but it doesn't look like that's going to happen.

Despite getting a scholarship that covers full tuition at North Carolina University in Chapel Hill, I can't afford room and board. I can't even try to find a cheap place to rent because it's a policy for Freshman to live on campus. Though I've been putting away money for years, my meager savings would barely get me through the first semester.

What would I do when the funds run out? Run back to Mama so she can make a mockery of me and get me back on the streets?

Maybe I can trick in Chapel Hill. There's gotta be good money there. Since it's part of the Research Triangle, there must be plenty of well-paid, powerful men who are bored with their wives and will pay for some fun.

I have to remind myself that it's better to have a concrete plan when the urge to go back to doing this envelops my thoughts. I'm going to college to get out of this life.

Maybe Drago here can help.

I feel stupid for not having thought things through before engaging with this Russian mobster. Instead of the tough act, I should have played the vixen from the start.

"Why don't you get a job?" Stan asks me, oblivious to the scheme brewing in my head.

"I get paid to go on dates with men. That is a job," I say, sounding a bit too cheery about it even for my taste.

"Hmm," is all he says in reply like, he is trying to assess me.

Stan's eyes never seem to leave my face; something I find both unnerving and exhilarating. The man has hazel eyes, not the stereotypical blue ones that I've heard many Europeans are blessed with. So what if he has a black heart? He's rich, and seems to have some sort of feelings for me.

On that note, it's time to be mysterious and announce my intention to leave. "As much as I'd love to continue this heart-warming conversation," I tell him, already moving to get out of the bed. "My mother probably thinks that I am dead in a gutter somewhere in a pool of blood."

"She might not be wrong if Waylon had given you to someone else."

A shiver shakes my entire body and causes my knees to buckle, but I swallow back the fear and continue.

"Goodbye, Stan." I pick up my dress in one hand and hold the soft, luxurious blanket against my chest. He doesn't make any move to get up, so I arch my brow expectantly. "Can you go into another room, so I can get dressed?"

"All right." He sighs and rolls his eyes like a teenager.

When he slides out of bed, he's completely naked. I've never seen anyone built like him. It's like he's been carved out of stone and tagged with black graffiti.

He walks up to me, towering over me so much I'm in his shadow. No one could look more menacing and macho as this specimen staring into my eyes right now.

"I will see you soon, Katrina," he promises before entering the bathroom and closing the door.

Excitement pools in my core as my brain goes into overdrive, fantasizing about all the things his words could mean.

Chapter Five

HARRIS

THE IMAGE of the lady in red from the other night keeps appearing in my thoughts.

Katrina; her name still echoes in my mind. Most times I take note of people out of habit and tuck it away, but this girl is a recurring memory .

Why? What makes her so special? I ask myself as I commute to work on this wet Monday. It rained nonstop last night and I don't even know if we'll be able to work, but I didn't get a call, so I'm dragging my ass to the job site just in case.

"I'm Kat," her voice echoes in my head again as I pull my truck into a parking spot across the street from the site.

Her demeanor held a curious mix of independence and innocence wrapped in a gorgeous, petite frame. I'm tempted to ask Beau about her, but I'm concerned because he introduced her to Waylon.

Why would he do that? I hope she realized what a scumbag he is and got away from him quickly.

If Beau and shady Waylon hadn't interrupted us, perhaps I would've had the chance to get to know her better. I have a knack for being a good judge of character and I have a feeling Katrina is a damn smart girl. That's what made me go against my urge to ignore her.

When you spend most of your life being an average student, you tend to have a radar for picking out smart people. Befriending the right people helped me pass more than a few classes over the years.

I jump out of my truck and stuff my keys into the front pocket of my jeans.

I didn't even sleep with her. Beau and Waylon whisked her away before we could even have a proper conversation, and when they returned, she wasn't with them. So why has she occupied every waking thought?

The smell of cheap lavender assaults my senses. My head snaps up to the woman passing me on the sidewalk. It takes me a moment to realize it isn't Katrina, they just happen to share the same taste in fragrance. As unrefined as the perfume smells, it lingers.

"My grandmother would say I've been bewitched," I mutter under my breath. "Maybe she's an enchantress."

I pause and glance around to see if anyone heard me.

Instead of talking to myself and sniffing random women on the street, it's time to stop daydreaming about a girl I'll never see again and focus on the job.

And the shit I'm about to take for blowing off Colt and the boys on Friday night. The thought of it makes me groan.

"Mornin', Miss. Betty," I greet the older black woman at the front desk of the pop-up office on the work site as I slide my card into the time clock.

"Good mornin', Harris," she replies. "You have a good weekend?"

"I did, thanks for asking. How's Mr. Tucker feeling?"

"Oh, you know how it is for us old folk, Harris." She smiles. "Aches and pains all the time, but we thank the Lord we wake up in the morning and push through another day."

"Amen!" I smile and tip my baseball cap to her. Miss Betty has been working for Commons for as long as I can remember. Despite being in her sixties, she's still sharp as a tack. All the foremen want her on their project.

When I head out to the building, I see Colt and a few guys standing around sipping coffee and talking, just as we do every morning. I walk toward the group in long strides, hoping they aren't too pissed.

"Mornin', Harris," Colt says, stretching out his hand for a shake. "Sorry, we couldn't make it to the bar on Friday." He lowers his head. "I didn't have your number, so I didn't know how to get ahold of you."

It takes a lot of willpower to not let the relief show on my face, then I do the most natural thing anyone would do; play along.

"Yeah, I got there a little after nine and couldn't help but wonder where everyone was," I reply, looking disturbed.

Lying comes fairly easy to me since my entire life around the guys is a lie. I'm always making things up or trying to remember what I said previously so I keep my story straight. Thankfully, I'm young enough to have a fairly simple backstory.

"Tony's wife passed on Friday," Colt replies solemnly, sounding genuinely hurt by the death of our colleague's spouse.

"Oh no. He's not coming in today, is he?" I ask looking around.

"Nah. He had to drive home to upstate New York to make funeral arrangements," Raphael answers. "Poor guy. They had barely begun their life as a couple and he's gotten the rug pulled out from under him."

"He must be devastated," I say, unable to process what the death of a loved one feels like.

I imagine it'll hit me hard when Granddaddy passes. He's not the stereotypical cute, cuddly grandfather sneaking us candy. He's a self-made billionaire whom I look up to with god-like reverence, especially when he sneaks me a shot of whiskey.

Granddaddy traveled the state expanding his empire and giving us philosophical talks about family and discipline. He was a true visionary —and when a visionary gives you advice, you take it. Technically, he's retired, but he still has his hand in everything Commons Property Development does.

"Alright, gentleman. Pull your panties up!" Colt announces. "It's time to get to work."

"Here we go," I mutter under my breath as I strap on my tool belt, pushing Tony's loss and Katrina's memory out of my mind.

Chapter Six

COOKIE

MAMA HAD BEEN furious about my late arrival back at the apartment, but I didn't care.

Since my encounter with Stan, life has been a little more colorful. Almost like a glimmer of hope has given me the ability to see with rose-colored glasses.

Even Mama's gritty behavior seems to get to me less these days. She must notice because she keeps making weird comments like:

"Men don't love women. They take what they can get from us and toss us out like yesterday's trash. You best remember that, Katrina!"

Or:

"There's no such thing as love. A good relationship is when you find a man who takes care of you without beating you."

I don't understand why she keeps bringing up love, because I never mentioned the word. I'm certainly not in love with Stan. Sure, he's gorgeous and sexy in an intriguing, dangerous way. But I can't get involved with someone in the mafia—even one who claims he wants to leave and make a fresh start in America.

There's also the pesky fact that I can't get the cute boy from Mangione's out of my head. I still wish *he* would have been my date on

Friday night, but I'm not that lucky. I get hooked up with gross, old men and Russian gangsters.

I already know there's no such thing as love. She's taught me that for years—not just in her rhetoric about men, but in how she treats me. It's not romantic love, of course, but she can't possibly love me.

No one can save me. Not her, not the Russian, not any man.

I'm the only one who can save myself from the mental torture of our pitiful life. I'm the only one who can give myself a better situation.

If only she knew what I'm planning.

I have a real shot at attending NCU in the fall, and if Stan can help me get there, I'm doing everything in my power to make it happen.

Mama doesn't realize that we have the same dream. We both want me to marry a rich man, have kids, and live happily ever after—whatever that is. But because Mama never went to college, she doesn't realize that's where the men are.

North Carolina University is the premiere college in the state. All the rich kids go there—or Duke University—which is a town or two over.

At college, I'll have a chance to meet someone *and* get an education. Either way, it'll get me out of poverty. I don't want to depend on someone. If I marry rich, fine, let him take care of me and fawn over me and buy me all the things—but I'm going to have a hand in whatever business my future-husband is a part of. I refuse to be left with nothing if the marriage doesn't work.

When the phone rings on Tuesday morning, I'm not surprised when it's Waylon Harding telling me that Stan wants to meet up with me again. The thing that surprises me is why it took so long. He directs me to meet the Russian at Eastland Mall after school.

"Hook, line, and sinker," I whisper as I hang up the phone. Giddiness makes bubbles flutter in my stomach. Maybe my plan isn't too far-fetched after all.

As soon as I hang up, I rush to tell Mama immediately – saying that one of my clients wants to buy us clothing, jewelry, and makeup. It's always best to lay it on thick.

"Mama!" I call, rushing to her. She's on the couch watching the local news. "Mama! Guess what?"

"What's all the fuss, Katrina?" She takes a drag on her cigarette.

"Remember the man from Friday night—the one you said was a good one?" I plop down next to her and grab her hand, playing up my excitement.

"Yeah?"

"He wants to take me to *Eastland* Mall after school," I say, emphasizing Eastland because it's the biggest and best mall in Charlotte. "He wants to buys me clothes and jewelry and makeup!" I squeeze her hand.

"Really?" she asks.

I've never seen her look as proud of me than she is at this minute. She's always pounded it into my head that the best thing was to find one man and milk him for all I could before moving on.

My mind has been reeling with so many thoughts over the past few days that the only thing that keeps me grounded is Stan and the thought of what he can offer.

During school, all I can think about is my meeting with the beautiful, dangerous Russian who occupies my mind.

Dre catches my eye a few times during English class. I smile sheepishly and lift my fingers in a slight wave. I can't help the guilt that washes over me. After years of telling him everything, this plan is one thing I can't reveal. It's too dangerous to tell anyone.

The last thing I want is for the Russian mafia to shake down my best friend for answers about me. My life is what it is, Dre's doesn't have to be affected by it.

After enduring hours of different teachers droning on about the topic they would repeat to the next batch of 12th graders, I finally get to leave school and get to the adventurous part of the day. I am curious to find out what the Russian has in store for me; probably more sex and some money for me to keep on the side.

At least, that's what I'm hoping.

I pick out a pair of faded, straight-leg jeans that hold my butt firmly and peg them at the ankle. Then, I slip on a hot pink crop top that exposes my flat, toned belly. It's flirty, but still leaves enough for the imagination.

Today, I'm the seductress, and I plan on sinking my claws completely in Stan.

Mama taught you well, a voice says in my head and I can't help but feel ashamed. But this is what I have to do to reach my goals.

My knees shake and I'm on the edge of my seat while the bus weaves through Charlotte streets on the way to Eastland. When I walk in, I feel a twinge of jealousy when I spot other girls who look to be around my age, giggling and having fun.

I'm not jealous they're having fun. I'm jealous because I missed out on that part of life. I never got to hang out at the mall with friends like I didn't have a care in the world. I didn't have the money—or the time. I can't remember what it feels like to have such innocence and freedom.

Freedom. The same thing Stan's looking for in America.

As if he knows I'm thinking of him, I look up and watch as he descends from the escalator like a hovering angel. He smiles when his eyes focus on my face.

I note the way his skin crinkles around his eyes. Stan might look like a kindly old man when he ages, which is a weird juxtaposition seeing as he's probably committed more than one murder in his time on earth. For some reason, his dangerous past and his rugged handsomeness allures, rather than frightens, me. Which definitely confirms how messed up I am.

Stan is dressed in a way that compliments his rugged looks; a pair of loose, off-white pants with a round-necked shirt tucked into them and a crème jacket to top it off. Looking at him, you would think he stepped out of a men's fashion magazine.

"Katrina," he greets me, opening his arms for an embrace that I didn't expect. When I hesitate, he gently pulls me into his arms. Can a Mafioso be gentle?

The warmth comforts me immediately. I breathe in the scent of nutmeg, oranges, and cinnamon and relax into his embrace. The memory of his naked body flashes through my head, and sparks throbbing between my legs.

"You look beautiful," he says when we pull apart. I feel light-headed and giddy again and it isn't just because of this man's money and how it can help me, it's something different.

Stan makes a circle with his arm and offers it to me. After I loop mine in his, he places his palm over my hand and holds it across his stomach. It's much more intimate than holding hands—which is really awkward when the height difference is immense like ours is.

Together, we explore the mall. We walk silently, save for the times I point out something to teach him about American culture.

He stops abruptly in front of a jewelry store, staring at a simple silver necklace with a solitaire diamond so intently I'm worried that he might be thinking of robbing the store and making me his accomplice.

"This will look good on you," he says haltingly in that sexy Russian accent. I snort out a laugh taking his words as a joke, but Stan's flat expression doesn't change. Suddenly, he smiles mischievously and pulls me toward the door.

"No, no, no," I protest when I realize what he's up to. This man will get me killed.

"Come on, I get you one," he says stubbornly, pulling me toward the entrance again.

"Stan. Listen to me for a minute," I say sharply, trying to dig my feet into the slippery concrete floor. Surprisingly enough, he stops to listen. "Someone will mug me or kill me if I wear something that expensive in my part of Charlotte."

Stan's muscles tighten under my grip and he narrows his eyes. "What is mug?" he asks but I have a feeling that the other words have gotten under his skin.

"They will rob me," I explain.

"I would break such person," Stan quips.

I know he's not joking, but why would he want to seek revenge and risk incarceration again for my sake. Maybe he's taken a liking to me, but I can't risk making such assumptions yet. I need to solidify his affection before he gets bored and tosses me aside for fresher meat.

"I know you will," I agree, trying to play on his ego. "But please, no jewelry. My own mother would take it and pawn it for cash."

In fact, that's the most likely scenario. She's done it before.

Stan's eyes lock with mine and we have a staring contest until he gives in—another surprising thing for him to do. I'd expected him to stand his ground.

"*Da*. All right." He sighs in resignation. "Then I buy you something else."

He takes me into another store. One with clothing so expensive, I know even one item on the rack would probably pay our rent for the next quarter. For some reason it makes me uncomfortable, which means I need to suck it up and work harder at this gold-digging gig.

How am I supposed to get money from him when I cringe at the idea of him spending it on me?

Maybe because it feels like he's looking out for me, and I've never had that before.

Stan and I walk through the store. He's very patient, waiting as I stop every few steps and riffle through a rack of clothes.

"I wish there was a store that had affordable clothes that were still fashionable," I mutter while flipping through a rack of the beautiful— yet grossly overpriced—dresses. "Everything is either ridiculously expensive or cheap and ugly."

"What does this matter?" he asks. "You do not pay for this."

"I know, Stan. I just"—I shake my head—"I feel weird about letting you spend this much money on me. Especially since you're going back to Moscow soon. And—I don't know. I'm the worst prostitute ever." I laugh.

Men like Stan don't care about other people's feelings. The plan mulling through my head has me paranoid. I don't know how much time I have to charm him. All the while these thoughts are crossing my mind, Stan's been watching me intently and from his expression, I realize that for the first time in a long while, I've let my poker face drop.

"You know why I bring you here today?" he asks, gesturing for me to sit me on a bench outside of the fitting rooms. The action earns us an ugly look from the woman at the till. I'm guessing it's because we haven't brought any clothes to try on. She must not be happy we've suddenly converted the store into a meeting place.

"No, Stan, I have no idea," I reply with my arms folded, trying to harden my resolve and brace myself for the worst.

Stan sweeps a stray lock of hair away from my face and tucks it behind my ear. Why is he acting like this is some sort of romance novel? Where's the blunt man I opened up to on Saturday?

"I want you to stop prostitution," he says, gazing into my eyes.

I feel like he flipped my world upside down. What is he talking about? Then, I do the dumbest thing and laugh out loud, earning us another nasty look from the lady at the register. Stan glowers at her so harshly it makes goosebumps pop up on my arms. The violence inside him is barely bridled.

But when he turns back me, his face softens until he looks worried. "I need to get you out of this situation before it too late," he continues calmly.

The possibility of Stan helping me get out of prostitution fills me with hope. At my current rate, I'd never be able to get to Chapel Hill.

It would be nice to finally stop being sold to different men. It would be nice to not have my gag reflex tripped when I walk by someone wearing expensive cologne and not be reminded of the disgusting, sweaty men as they cover my body, pumping in and out until they collapse in a heap on top of me.

The hope crumbles almost as fast as it rose.

"If I quit, how am I'm supposed to survive and take care of my mother?" I ask.

"I will take care of you," he says, taking my hand in his.

I can imagine Mama's reaction to those words. She would probably dance around and laugh with glee until the aftermath of too many cigarettes gets her coughing and hacking.

"Why?" I ask again. "Is this because of your mother and sister?"

A pained expression crosses his face but he recovers quickly. That nerve must be rawer than I realize. "Yes, but there is another reason," he says, his voice hoarse now.

Oh Lord, please don't cry, I say in silent prayer. I never thought I would ever see Stan be so emotional.

"You are in my heart, Katrina."

I bite my lip as I process his words. He obviously knows what to say to sweep a girl off her feet. But at the same time, the admission scares me. I wanted him to keep me around long enough to get me to UNC, but I didn't realize he had feelings for me.

And what scares me even more is that I have feelings for the hazel-eyed criminal sitting next to me.

A proper, Southern girl should be crushing on rock stars or actors or the cute boy in her Science class. But here I am swooning over Russian Mafioso. Proving there's nothing proper about me.

"And that man," Stan continues, oblivious to my internal turmoil. "That Waylon Harding—he is not good person. He is dangerous. Your mother do not know what he capable of."

This part grabs my attention more than anything else. "What are you talking about," I ask.

"Waylon Harding is sex trafficker," Stan explains. "I come from Russia and act like a client, which is how I meet you. Information I have, say that it is Waylon Harding's people who kidnap my sister and bring her to America."

"Oh my god," I say through an exhale.

What has Mama gotten me into?

"He traffic girls, hook them on drugs, and turn them to prostitute that he controls," he continues with his explanation. "After I done with you, he will force you to use much heroin. You will be addict and do anything he say for next fix. You be in Mexico before sundown."

My chest tightens, making it harder and harder to breathe. The hate for my mother that's always been bubbling at the surface, intensifies, threatening to spill over. I don't trust her enough to know whether or not she knew about all this. Mama has always been calculating, but could she have stooped this low?

"You are lucky I am first client he give you," Stan says. He's still next to me, but it sounds like he's a million miles away. "Don't worry, Katrina. I will take care of the situation. I will take care of you."

"I need some air," I say, scrambling off the bench and running out of the store into the concourse.

Chapter Seven

COOKIE

I CAN'T HELP but fume as I head back home. The bus ride back is quiet, thank God for that. The droning of the engine is calming—almost therapeutic—but it doesn't drown out the questions floating around in my brain.

What kind of mother does that sort of thing? I've been trying to come up with a plausible excuse as to why Mama would set me up with a sex trafficker.

What would have happened to me if I was given to another client who has no personal interest? Would I be hooked on heroin and look like one of those junkie hookers on the corner of Trade and Tryon?

More importantly, what the hell am I supposed to do now? Can I trust Stan to be true to his word about protecting me?

Skepticism begins to rear its ugly head, but I remind myself that I wouldn't have all the information I do right now if Stan hadn't shared it with me. I don't think he would share that information if his intention was doing me harm.

But what if he's a sadistic psychopath who's showing me all the cards because it's more fun for him?

He *is* mafia, after all.

No. I doubt he would have let me leave if that were the case.

At this point, I feel like I'll explode from the overload of thoughts. Thankfully, the bus stops and I get off quickly. The need to question Mama grows stronger with every step I take toward our apartment building. I pray I don't murder her by the time the day is done.

Stan's words echo in my mind. *"Don't worry, Katrina. I will take care of the situation. I will take care of you."*

I don't talk to anyone as I walk into the building. Thankfully, Dre wasn't outside when I got home because I'm sure I would've snapped at him if he tried to start up a conversation. I have enough problems, I don't want to add having my best friend pissed at me to the laundry list.

"Mama!" I shout before I even close the door behind me, scanning the room for her. "Mama!"

There's silence in the apartment until I hear the toilet flush, and I realize she's been in the bathroom.

Mama steps out with a scowl on her face which means she'll have something scathing to say but right now I do not care.

"I don't know what's come over you to think that you can scream my name all over my house," she counters. I look around what she calls a 'house', but all I see is a seedy room in a rundown building.

"How dare you set me up with a sex trafficker!" I bellow at her, ignoring her question.

"What the hell are you talkin' about, Katrina?" Mama fires back. "And you best watch your mouth before I smack it, you hear? I'm your mother, and you will respect me."

"Do you know what Waylon Harding does?" I ask, ignoring her threats.

All I get in return is a blank stare like she's expecting me to divulge more information. "Who's that?"

Is she playing with me or has this woman lost her mind? Again.

"The man you set me up with on Friday, Mama. Waylon Harding," I explain calmly, trying not to come off as a raging lunatic.

"I don't know any Waylon Hard-on or whatever name you said. I set you up with a handsome man named Beau Commons whose family owns most of the city. I told him that my daughter was the finest piece of ass in town." She scowls, but it's quickly wiped away when she starts coughing. Between hacks, she glares at me. "I told you not to fuck it up with him. Did you fuck it up?"

Instead of trying try to figure out why I'm so upset, she's angry because she thinks I've ruined her trip to Easy Street. It breaks my heart but steels my resolve to leave her as soon as I have the chance.

I've always second guessed her love, but now I know for certain— my mother doesn't give two shits about me. She's a lazy piece of trash with no education and low self-esteem who prostituted herself to make money. I've always been an obligation, not a daughter. Until I turned sixteen when I became a slave.

What bothers me now is the confusion at hand. Was it Beau— Harris' brother—who set me up to be trafficked? Or was he oblivious of the whole thing? Is Stan lying to me so I have to play the damsel in distress and depend on him?

More questions pile up in my mind, but my train of thought gets derailed when the phone rings. I rush to it, grabbing the lime green receiver and answering breathlessly.

It's Waylon saying he wants to see me immediately. There's a new client he wants me to meet who won't be in town for long.

Fear grapples me as I write down the address on a sheet of paper.

I could say no. But then what would he do? Kidnap me? Drug me? Send me to Mexico?

Kill me?

"Only one way to find out," I say out loud. I make one more call before I grab the paper and storm out of the apartment.

"Where do you think you're going?" Mama calls as I rush past her.

I don't answer—don't even turn around.

THE ADDRESS LEADS me to a small warehouse off Westinghouse Blvd, which makes me feel uneasy, but I keep moving.

Upon entering, it looks like a makeshift bar has been constructed and the exterior was left that way to make the place inconspicuous. A cover, so to speak.

"Ah, Katrina, there you are," Waylon's voice booms sounding more like he is announcing my presence than welcoming me.

I follow the sound and spot him sitting with another man around the left side of the bar. They wear suits like they are legitimate businessmen—maybe bankers, but now I know better; it's all a disguise.

"Seems like you've become a bit of a superstar, darling," he drawls as I get to where he and his partner sit. After a quick look around, I count five men scattered around the space. If I'm being set up to die there's no way I'll be able to escape.

My stomach drops. I'm totally screwed, but I keep the unease from reaching my face.

"I just try to keep clients happy," I say, trying to sound neutral. It's not hard to achieve, since I steel myself—almost like turning into another persona when I do what I do and talk about what I do.

"You do more than keep them happy, Katrina," he argues. "You drive them wild. That Russian for instance, he's is always calling for more. You must have a magical pussy."

Bile rises in my throat, but I just shrug. "What can I say?" I ask, sliding my lips into a sultry smile.

Though, I'm not too flattered at the idea of being North Carolina's most wanted prostitute, playing it up seems like my best plan of action after being told I have a magic pussy. I assume that's how he wants me to react.

"Oh, pardon my manners," he says suddenly, pointing to the ceiling as if he's just remembered something. "Please have a seat."

He motions to a small table with one chair. I do as he says because being too uptight isn't going to save me from these sharks.

"Drink?" he asks, looking earnest and polite—a thorough gentleman.

"Just water, please," I reply, my voice suddenly hoarse.

Waylon tilts his head, arching one eyebrow as he studies me. Then he gestures to someone behind the bar who was practically within earshot. He lights a stucco cigar as the bartender pours water into a glass for me. It's no surprise I know about cigars. When you hang around enough old men you get to know these things.

I lift the cup to my lips, but don't drink. Waylon slipped something into my champagne the night I met him. I'm not falling for the same trap this time.

The second man, who Waylon hasn't introduced me to, gets up and walks past me. It takes everything in me to not to jump up and try my luck at bolting out of this place.

As I contemplate turning to see what the man is up to, Waylon speaks up after a long exhale of smoke.

"I can tell that you and I are going to get along just fine," he starts, his words sounding more like a warning than a business agreement. He gets up, flipping his Zippo lighter between his thumb and forefinger. He cradles his cigar in his left hand, accentuating the gold ring set with a huge ruby on his pinky finger.

"There's just a little matter of insurance, you see?" he drawls walking into my field of vision, filling it.

My body tenses immediately. Hands grab me before I can react. My heart races so fast and hard it feels like it might burst before they have their way with me. Stan was right about this bastard.

I scream out and struggle but more hands hold me down against the chair.

"It's nothing personal, darling, just business," Waylon says, stepping back. "Don't worry. You're gonna feel real good after this."

All I see is another person—the man who had been sitting with him when I arrived, I believe—coming toward me with a syringe in his hand.

"Please, please, don't do this, please." Those are the only words I can get out, as he stalks closer, holding the syringe up and flicking the needle.

I close my eyes and brace for the pain but instead, loud gunshots echo through the room and chaos ensues.

I roll off the chair and dive under the couch beside me. The sound of rapid gunfire and shouting fills the air.

"Katrina!" I hear the muffled sound of my name through ringing ears. "Katrina!" The voice calls out more urgently.

When I look up, Stan pulls me from my hiding spot and takes me into his arms. After a heart-pounding minute to clear my head, I punch him on the chest.

"That was close, you jerk," I complain, punching him on the chest again, but I'm relieved that he came through or my life would be taking a different turn right now.

Stan chuckles and leads me through the room, weaving around bodies on the floor twisted into funny angles with blood leaking out of them. The sight makes me want to vomit.

When I look around, I notice multiple men holding rifles, ready to shoot, but since they aren't, I assume they're with Stan. I don't know whether to feel relived or more frightened being surrounded by what has to be more Russian mafia.

Then I see Waylon.

He's being held down in a chair looking like he shit himself. I've never been happier to see someone in distress. I break Stan's hold on me and rush to Waylon, slapping him, punching him, raking my nails across his face—anything to inflict as much pain as I possibly can.

No one stops me until Stan comes over to stand next to me. For the first time, I notice the large pistol in his hand.

"For my sister—and my love," he says before placing the gun on Waylon's temple and pulling the trigger. Bone, brains, and blood spray across the floor.

I scream and cover my eyes, dry heaving and hyperventilating as I try to regain composure.

Maybe this is normal for Stan, but it's not for me. I've never witnessed any kind of death—let alone multiple people murdered in a shootout right before my eyes.

I touched Waylon. What will I say to the police? I wipe my hands across my jeans repeatedly almost as if in a trance.

"Let's go." Stan's voice is hard as he gestures at the bodies sprawled around the room with his pistol hand. When he pulls me toward the door, the only thing I can do is allow myself to be led away.

Chapter Eight

COOKIE

I'VE NEVER BEEN a fan of surprises. Maybe it's because I've never had a positive one. So, when Stan breaks the news that he needs to return to Moscow, I don't take it in stride.

"When will you be back?" I ask, praying that my voice won't betray me as my eyes fill with tears. If I blink too quickly, the waterworks will start.

"As soon as I can," he says, holding my face in his palms. Tears spill onto my cheeks and roll down. Stan wipes them off with his thumbs. His expression is almost as pained as mine.

We both know marriage isn't an option. Not only because we've only known each other for two weeks, but also because of his ties to the mafia. I'd be used as a tool to hurt him if the need arises and Stan refuses to let that happen.

"That's not a time frame," I reply, sniffling.

"I don't have a better answer, my sun. I have work in my country. Once I get everything sorted out. I will be back. This I promise you," he assures me but the realist in me doesn't believe any of it.

"You're leaving the mafia, right? No more crime? No more killing?" I ask, knowing my hopes will most likely be shattered. Stan shakes his head sadly, and I know what that means.

"Katrina." He takes a deep breath and lifts his eyes to the sky. "Is more complicated. You know this."

I swallow and nod, but a sob escapes my lips. I do know. It's not easy to stop doing what makes you money—and leaving the mafia is almost impossible.

Still, I believe he'll come back to me.

"What am I going to do without you?" I whisper.

"What you have always done—live." He brushes the feathery bangs out of my eyes, but the locks drop right back into place. It brings a gentle smile to his face. "They are as unruly as you."

I'm surprised laughter is able to escape my lips through the sobbing.

"How will I contact you?" I ask, desperate for answers, stability, something.

"There is no way. Is too dangerous. You know this, Katrina," he says. "But I have this for you." He reaches into his back pocket and pulls out a checkbook. It looks foreign to me; checkbooks aren't something I'm accustomed to seeing regularly. Food stamps, on the other hand, are a constant.

"Do not go back to your mother. You must get a job as we discussed," Stan continues, sounding more frantic by the second. "You will use this money to find place to rent and pay the bills. When I come back, I will buy the building and start my business."

The certainty of his tone gives me hope, and the access to his account gives me even more.

"I can't take your money," I say, earning me one of those pained looks he usually has on his face when I do something that hurts him.

The way he glares at me would scare anyone, but I'm not afraid. A menacing look is all he'd ever do to me; I can't say the same for anyone else.

"You can take the money from strangers, but not money offered by someone who cares about you and wants you to get out of this situation?" The words pack a heavy punch but I know he is just trying to manipulate me into taking the checkbook.

"Yes. It's completely different, Stan. I don't care about the guys that give me the money or the gifts. They are nothing," I start, keeping my voice as level as possible. "I don't want to take your money. You've helped me and cared for me. I see a future with you."

My heart beats faster. A reminder that it's a lie, just like all the other lies. I'll take his money—his help. Though I do feel more for him that I have for anyone I've been with, he's a means to get what I want —just like all the others.

If he gets his rocks off thinking he's saving me, let him think that way. If he wants to give me money to get me out of my mother's house, I'll take it. But I'm not a stereotypical damsel in distress that needs a man to save her. I can save myself.

My plan has always been to scrape up enough money to get out from under my mother's thumb as soon as I graduate from high school.

Maybe he thought I was going to let her pimp me out forever. Maybe he still thinks I'm stupid like he told me I was on the day we met.

When I close the door on that nasty, roach-infested apartment for the last time, I will never, ever be back.

"You care for me, yes?" Stan asks earnestly.

"You know how much." I nod, flashing him a sexy smile and curling my fingers around his neck.

"I don't know this." He bats my hand away. "You treat me the same way you treat all men."

Rejected, I step back. I want to feel hurt by his words but there are no lies in them. "Then why give me money? Why keep the cycle going? Just leave and don't look back!" I spit because he is driving me nuts.

"Because I don't want you to go to other men for things. If you need anything, I will be the man who provides," he replies sharply.

"You want to provide for me even though you think I'm using you?" This back and forth is giving me a headache, but I'm a fan of clarity so these questions have to be asked.

"Of course, you're using me, Katrina," he replies, throwing his hands up in exasperation. "It is all you know. Change take a longer time than a few weeks."

The fact that he knows what I'm doing sobers me when I thought I was a master manipulator. What's that old saying? It takes one to know one.

If he realizes I'm using him to get away from my mother and make a better life for myself and he's okay with it, then I'm not going to argue with him.

"As long as you understand," I say, plucking the checkbook from his hands.

He grabs my hips and pulls me toward him. Then he places one hand around my neck and lifts my head until our eyes meet.

"You can pretend that I am nothing, but I know better. I can smell your desire. I can feel your heart race when I'm close. I know your panties get soaked every fucking time I put my hands on you," he whispers as he lowers his lips to my ear.

When I swallow hard, my throat presses against his hand.

"I guarantee I am the only man who has ever made you feel that way," he adds. I would laugh at those words if they came from someone else but, again, there are no lies with Stan.

He's not wrong. I want his money, sure, but there's an unbridled lust I can't shake. I can't deny the way he makes me feel. Or the longing in my heart when he's not with me. Instead of responding with words, I rise to my tiptoes and press against him, reaching to cover his mouth with mine. He releases my throat and allows me the pleasure.

Our lips collide with bruising pressure, and he slides his tongue into my open mouth, teasing and prodding until my tongue reaches out. He closes his mouth and sucks. When he lets go, his teeth rake across my lips and he bites the lower one, holding it until I whimper but even then, he doesn't let up.

I know him too well to know that he won't let go until we're a pile of limp limbs and forgotten dreams, broken and sweaty on the floor. He grabs my hair at the base of my neck and tugs on the roots, pulling my head back so I'm at the angle he wants to devour me.

My hands claw at his sides until my nails sink into the inked skin of his torso. I never knew what I was missing until him. I never knew sex could be enjoyable or that a man could take me in such a rough, demanding way and have it provoke excitement and desire, rather than fear.

These were the last things I remember before sliding into pleasure-filled bliss.

Chapter Nine

COOKIE

IT'S BEEN three months since Stan left for Russia, and even with the beautiful Carolina sun shining on my face every day, life still seems dull and colorless.

When he left, I started having nightmares about the day Waylon tried to inject me with whatever drug was in that syringe. Instead of try to fall back to sleep, I put all those extra waking hours into focusing on my studies. I ended up graduating as the salutatorian of my class. Which isn't as great as valedictorian, but it's a step up from being third place.

Suck it, Stan.

Mama and I fought all summer mostly because I stopped taking clients and got a job at the convenience store down the road, but also because I chopped off my hair. I went from sexy Farrah Fawcett waves to Princess Di posh. She wasn't amused at my royal makeover, which means I made the right choice. Now, she shuffles around mumbling about how ungrateful I am and how she wishes I were never born between hacking coughs. According to her, I ruined her life.

Funny thing is, I agree.

Stan still hasn't come back—or contacted me. Sometimes, the thought of him crosses my mind without warning, and I can't help but feel depressed. I owe him my life, and he's halfway across the world now. Sometimes I feel like ripping his checkbook apart but I can't because knowing he's getting me to NCU is the only thing that keeps me going and it's the only thing I have left of him.

It hurts, but I'm doing what he told me to do. I'm living.

Which is why I'm roaming around Walkins Gymnasium in a daze trying to snag the classes I need for my first semester at North Carolina University. If I would have realized what a complete and total shit-show registration would be, I would've gotten here much earlier.

The only way to describe the scene is complete chaos. Thousands of students pushing and shoving, trying to get to tables lined up around the room to grab a slip of paper for the class they need. I would have thought a school this prestigious would have a much better system.

But here we are, rushing around frantically, throwing elbows, and praying a few kind souls trade for a class you need.

"What are you looking for?" A cute guy in a grey sweater calls out, disrupting my shuffling around with eyes as wide as a deer-in-the-headlights. For some reason he looks slightly familiar, but I can't place him. He's got his arm up, waving coveted slips of paper in the air.

"English Lit with Malcolm!" I call across the crowd.

"Got it! Hang on. Let me come your way." He edges through the group.

"Hey," he says as he reaches me.

"Hey," I say, giving him a shy smile.

"English Lit with Malcolm is pretty popular. I grabbed a few when I was over there." He hands me the paper I need.

"Thank you so much." I hold the paper to my heart, so excited, I could practically kiss him. Instead, I scan his face again, trying to figure out how I know him.

"What'cha got for me, gorgeous?" He nods to the papers in my hand.

"What?" I ask, distracted by the compliment as warmth spreads in my stomach.

"Do you have a class to trade for that English Lit I just gave you.

That's kind of the way this works." He flashes me a smile which reveals brilliant, straight white teeth.

"Oh, yeah. Um, I have these." I hand him the extra papers in my hand—the ones I don't need for my schedule.

He riffles through them. "These are crappy classes, Sugar," he says laughing. Even his laughter sounds like music.

"I got here late. Didn't quite understand the process," I say, shrugging.

"Yeah, it's crazy. My brother went here, so he gave me the insider tip," he says, adjusting the strap of his backpack.

"You look familiar," I say, unable to contain the feeling that we've met before.

"Are you from Charlotte?" he asks.

"Born and raised."

"Maybe wave crossed paths," he offers. "Did you go to Myers Park?"

"No." I shake my head, mentally trying to figure out how to avoid telling him which high school I went to when I suddenly realize how I recognize his face.

He was at Mangione's having drinks with his brother the night I met Waylon. He was there right before Waylon took me to Stan.

My heart speeds up as flight mode kicks in. I'm never going to be able to keep any story straight if I tell him under this kind of mental duress.

"I, um, it was really awesome of you to give me that Lit class," I say with a shy smile, averting my eyes and backing away. Despite my sudden retreat, I hope he understands my gratitude is genuine. "Thanks."

"Wait! Can I get your name?" he calls after me. "Your number?"

I bolt away without looking back as my heart threatens to break free from my chest.

ON MONDAY MORNING, I edge past a few people and settle into a seat in one of the middle rows of Professor Malcolm's English Lit class. The auditorium is completely packed, which makes sense since it was so sought-after during registration.

Thank God for Harris.

After I grab a notebook and pen out of my backpack, I lean over and set it on the floor. When I sit back, there's a tap on my shoulder. I turn around and find myself face to face with Harris Commons.

"Hey, gorgeous," he greets me. "I've been looking for you since you dashed away. Am I that heinous?"

I can't help but laugh. "No." I whisper, then glance at the front of the room where our professor just entered and placed his suitcase on the desk.

"Maybe I can get your digits."

"No," I whisper again before turning around and ignoring any other attempts to get my attention.

Over the next few weeks, I try to avoid him, but it feels as if we're meant to meet again because we keep running into one another. To make things worse, we share two of the same classes and he lives on the floor above me in the dorm.

One time, he even tried to send messages through the vent in the ceiling.

When my roommate found it, she tossed it to me, saying, "I'm pretty sure this is from the dude in three-oh-seven who won't stop trying to get your attention."

I unfolded the paper, laughing when I saw a note straight out of elementary school—written in handwriting that looked like it was from the same time frame.

Do you want to hang out?
Check yes or no.

IT WAS CUTE—JUVENILE—BUT cute. Still, I crumpled the paper and tossed it in the trash. Harris knows what I used to do—how I made my money to get here. It's a big school with plenty of fish in the sea, I don't have to interact with him.

One day after Lit class, he walks toward me with purpose and fire in his eyes. If I bolt, I'll come off as a mega-bitch, so I opt to stand my ground and see what happens. It is not like he'd do anything to embarrass me in public.

Would he?

"Is something wrong?" he asks me straight up without observing any sort of nicety. I can't help but respect someone who gets straight to the point.

"Don't you take no for an answer?"

He holds his chin with his thumb and forefinger, as if thinking. "In certain circumstances, yes."

I swallow back the urge to run because we're going to have to get this conversation out of the way sometime. Might as well be now. "Don't you remember me?"

"Yeah, you're the hot, mysterious girl from registration who shot me down and embarrassed me royally." He winks, but I don't see any other sort of recognition register on his face.

I look around, lowering my voice before saying. "We met this summer at Mangione's—with Beau and Waylon?" Maybe pushing that button will kick start his memory.

"Oh Lord, that guy! If I never saw that dude again it would be too soon." He grimaces as if he just passed through a garbage chute. His eyes light up. "Wait! You're the lady in red. Katrina, right?" he asks, as if unsure of his answer.

"Sorry, I was a tad hammered," he continues apologizing quickly.

I can't help but laugh at him.

"Yes, I am Katrina—Kat," I answer with a laugh, though I should be on alert and wary of the potential threat. "What is your deal with Waylon Harding?"

"Harding. Ugh. I can't stand that creep," he says with a shudder and sour look on his face. "And his stupid arrival interrupted a conversation with one of the most beautiful and intriguing women I've ever met," he adds in a flirty tone.

"I thought he was a buddy of yours," I say, throwing out one more feeler. His contempt for Waylon is quite apparent, but you can never be too careful.

"Nah. He's one of my father's business associates, but I hadn't seen him since I was a kid. Barely even remember him. I just think it's so disgusting that he was always after young girls," Harris says. Then he looks up at me. "Oh shit. Katrina, I didn't mean—"

"It's okay. He's not my cup of tea, either. He creeped me out, too."

Together, we walk toward the door and into the hallway.

"Is that why you've been avoiding me?" he asks, holding the door open for me. "Because I was there that night?"

"Yeah, well, that night was a bad run-in with him, and I didn't want to be friends with anyone associated with him," I confess, surprising myself.

"Never. That guy's a huge piece of shit. I'm sorry my brother introduced you to him."

September in North Carolina is an absolutely perfect month. Temperatures are lower, but still warm and comfortable. The wind glides across my cheek, and rustles color-changing leaves hanging from the trees above us.

"What's that?" I ask, pointing at the blue Tupperware bowl in his hand, sidestepping his comment.

"Oh, just some cookies from Mama's second care package," he says, looking a bit embarrassed.

"Second?" I ask. We've only been at school for three weeks.

"Yeah, she's a bit much. But she makes phenomenal oatmeal chocolate chip cookies. Want some?" he offers.

It's a simple gesture but I can't help but feel happy. Harris is a total sweetheart.

Stan crosses my mind, but I shove the thought away easily. Stan had been raw and lust-filled and I don't even know if I will ever see him again.

Stan abandoned me.

Being with Harris feels different, like my heart is doing backflips and butterflies are fluttering in my stomach, just as it felt the night we met.

"Yes, please," I accept his invitation. Harris points at a huge rock close by and we sit. He opens the lid earnestly and passes the entire bowl to me. It's filled with bigger-than-average cookies—definitely homemade.

I haven't had a homemade cookie in years. Dre used to bring me a few whenever his mom made them, but she's been so busy recently, baking fell by the wayside.

Harris watches my face as I pick one up and begin to chew on it. The chocolate melting in my mouth makes me feel like I'm in heaven. I stop, finish chewing slowly, and swallow, uneasy at being watched as I eat. I pause before taking another bite.

"Don't stop, please. It's cute how much you love those cookies. My mother keeps sending them to me in care packages from home and I can only eat a few before I start hating the taste of them," he says making a face and I giggle, careful to not choke.

I toss the last piece into my mouth. "I happen to think they're delicious. Thank you for sharing," I say with a grateful glance.

"I'll bring you the entire batch next time. Glad to see a girl who eats. Most of the girls around here are so worried about their waistline," he says with an irritated look on his face. All of the sudden, his eyes widen as if remembering something. "But, I'm not talking about you. You're perfect. Your body, ya know? Eat what you want."

I laugh. "Don't worry, Harris. I didn't take offense."

"Good. I felt like a major dickweed for a minute there." He runs a hand through his sandy-blond hair. "So, how'd you get the name Kat?"

"I don't know, I think someone said it one time and it just sort of stuck." I shrug. "I never really liked it, but it's kinda cool to have a nickname."

"I can't call you Kat. It's too—" he pauses to think—"edgy. Kat sounds like a feral creature who skulks through alleys hunting for food in trash cans."

I swallow hard remembering how I'd said the same thing to Stan about his name *and* nickname. Now I realize how rude it was.

"I get your point," I reply tightly.

"Oh Lord, that's not what I meant," he apologizes immediately. "What's my deal? I finally get the chance to talk to the girl I'm crushing on and I can't say anything right."

Heat rises to my cheeks at the thought of being the girl he's 'crushing on.'

"Don't worry. I actually like it when people are brutally honest with me. I'm the same way."

He laughs and glances down at the Tupperware. Then he shakes it as if he's got an idea. "How about Cookie?"

"One is enough, but thank you."

"No! I mean, you can have another if you want." He pushes them toward me. "Maybe I can call you Cookie. You like them and it's cute."

"I see what you did there." I poke him in the side playfully.

He stops my fingers by grabbing my hand and holding it. "Cookie it is then?"

I nod, ecstatic to have my hand in his. This is what flirting and getting to know someone with no expectations feels like. This is 'normal.'

"Want to get dinner sometime, Cookie?" he blurts out suddenly.

"Absolutely."

My answer has him grinning like an idiot. It's cute. Wholesome.

His smile could almost make me forget the sins of my past and believe that I have the chance to start over. His smile could almost make me forget what I did to get here.

Not the prostitution; the theft.

Two days before I moved to Chapel Hill, I drained Stan's bank account and set up my own at a different bank here.

My stomach growls, showing its dissatisfaction at being teased with one cookie. Thankfully, Harris doesn't hear it.

Everything about the exchange and my time with him today has my heart flipping out. Never in a million years did I think Harris Commons would be interested in me.

This is my chance at happily ever after, and I'll do whatever it takes to keep him.

Chapter Ten

COOKIE

Harris knocks on my door at eight o'clock on the dot, which I appreciate. I believe time is one of the most valuable gifts you can give someone, and I like when people understand that.

Dressed in a white, button-down shirt and black slacks, he looks more like a young business owner than a college student. He exudes an aura of confidence and calm that makes him even more handsome. My belly turns to mush.

"You look amazing," he compliments, kissing me on both cheeks. He smells like citrus mingled with a hint of woodsy aftershave. I don't think there's anything phenomenal about my outfit; a simple Carolina-blue dinner dress and black flats.

He opens the door for me to climb into his car. The black Volvo 700 series looks like it was taken straight off the showroom floor, all black with black leather interior.

I knew he was from a wealthy family, but this car screams *status*. Harris must be the son of some rich industrialist or a bank executive, I'm not sure, but I'll find out more about him tonight. The idea of him coming from a rich, well-connected family makes him even more attractive, and I don't plan on letting him go.

The restaurant he picked is beautiful, not too upscale but not cheap.

"Harris Commons. Reservation for two."

"Of course. Right this way, sir," the waiter says before leading us to our table. Harris holds out a chair for me to sit first.

"Seriously, are you always this nice?" I ask, remembering how I asked him the same thing the first time we met.

"Mama raised me to be a gentleman," he replies with a grin. "So, Cookie," he begins after the waiter takes our orders and pours us some wine.

Harris tells him to leave the bottle. I'm surprised the waiter didn't card us, but maybe they know him or his family. Probably one of those perks of being wealthy that others don't receive.

"What part of Charlotte are you from?" he asks.

I can't tell Harris I'm a dirt-poor girl from Villa Heights. He'll never see me again, no matter how intrigued he is. So, I do the thing I do best; I lie. I've rehearsed the story multiple times in my head, but lying to someone I actually care about makes me nervous. Thankfully, I manage to keep my cool on the outside, even as my mind races.

"I stayed with my aunt in Plaza Midwood until I turned eighteen and had access to a small inheritance."

"By inheritance, I take it both of your parents have passed away," he asks, his voice filled with empathy.

My heart lurches. By inheritance, I mean the money I stole from my Russian Mafioso former lover. But I'm not telling him that.

"Yes," I say, lifting my wine glass and taking a small sip.

"I'm sorry, Cookie," he says, rubbing his thumb over my left hand as he encases it in both his. He drops the topic immediately, and I'm relieved.

"It's okay. I was really young."

I change the subject quickly, which makes both of us more comfortable.

Throughout dinner, we talk about different things ranging from music—Harris loves Classic Rock like Pink Floyd and The Rolling Stones—to movies and books. Having a normal, fun conversation with a man is a first for me. Since being at NCU, it seems like I've had so many "firsts."

First time living with roommates. First time going to a college party. First time going to a football game.

"What do you want to do after college?" Harris asks.

First time being asked what I want to do with my life after college. The question catches me off guard.

"I don't know exactly," I say, tucking a lock of hair behind my ear. "But I could see myself running a business. High-powered executive by day, wife and mother by night."

When I look up, there's a spark in Harris' eyes and a smile on his face. "I can absolutely picture that."

"How about you?" I ask as heat rises in my cheeks. "What do you want to do?"

"My family owns a property development company, and I'm supposed to work there after graduation," he says after he finishes chewing a bite of steak. He poises his fork over another piece. "But I want to do my own thing. Blaze my own trail and knock everyone's socks off, ya know?"

I nod as if I understand what it means to be part of a family that has high hopes for me.

He continues, "Beau's going to take over the company when Daddy retires, and I don't want to be the Captain's second in command."

"The Captain?" I interrupt him with a chuckle.

The creamed spinach we got to share is so good I want to pour the entire bowl down my throat. The entire meal is better than any meal I've ever eaten.

He laughs. "Yeah, that's what I call my brother because he's so freaking bossy. Loves being the leader—even when everyone knows it's the crew doing the work."

"So that's why you don't want to work with him," I say slowly as if putting puzzle pieces together. "You'll do all the work and he'll get all the credit."

Harris looks at me as if he can't believe what I said. He's silent for so long it starts to make me uncomfortable.

"Sorry, I—" I begin to apologize thinking I overstepped my boundaries.

"No!" He grabs my hand. "Cookie! You get it! No one understands. They think I'm an ungrateful jerk for not wanting to accept the amazing opportunity in my lap. But I have ambitions of my own. I want to shine."

"I do understand. I want to shine, too."

"People are gonna need sunglasses when they walk by us," he teases.

"Is this the first date of a future power couple?" I jest, going along with the joke.

"I hope so, Cookie. Because I haven't been able to get you out of my head since the first time we met."

"Wait a minute!" I hold up my hand. "You just said you haven't stopped thinking about me since the day we met, but you didn't even recognize me when we re-met here. Sounds like you're telling lies, Mister."

"It's not a lie! I swear. I didn't recognize you because you've had a makeover since then." He wiggles his finger around his head.

My hand flies to my new shorter 'do. "Whoops!" I laugh. "I'd forgotten about the change."

"For the record, you did seem familiar to me, I just couldn't place you. Harris Commons doesn't forget a beautiful face."

Harris Commons.

My head swirls with the information I've learned tonight, putting the pieces together. Harris Commons. His family owns a property development company. Commons Property Development is well-known in Charlotte.

The Commons are one of the oldest and wealthiest families in North Carolina.

Hot damn, I struck absolute gold with this one.

After dinner, Harris drives me back to our dorm; opening the door to the car for me to get out. He makes me feel like a princess, and I will make him my prince. Harris is my key to money, power, and connections—the things I've always wanted. Him being an amazing guy is icing on the cake.

Harris walks me to the front door, but doesn't follow me in even though he lives here, too.

"Aren't you coming in?" I ask.

He glances at his car. "Gotta run her over to the Freshman parking lot. I'll walk back."

I nod in understanding. He leans in, placing his lips on mine. I don't shy away from his soft, full lips. The kiss is slow and intense, almost electric, with the way he brushes his lips against mine.

So, this is what a kiss feels like when you're both into one another, I think breathlessly as I pull away.

"I'm glad we crossed paths again, Katrina," he whispers, running his thumb across my mouth. It feels like a million volts charge through my body. "Goodnight, gorgeous."

The new experience sets my soul on fire and overwhelms me with emotion. It's a feeling I've never experienced before. I can't control it when the unexpected happens—I start to cry.

"What's wrong?" Harris asks, confusion and concern twisting his face. "Was the kiss that bad?" he continues, making me laugh through my sobbing.

"No, you big goat," I say, punching him lightly on the shoulder. "I just—" I pause to gauge whether or not I'm making the right decision by opening my heart so quickly.

"Go ahead, Cookie," Harris urges me to go on. "You can talk to me."

"You're just so perfect," I say and I mean it.

"You took the words right out of my mouth because so are you," he says, brushing the tears away from my eyes. "Can I see you tomorrow?"

I nod happily, my heart pounding so hard, I'm afraid it might come out of my chest.

He leans in and pecks my cheek before bounding down the stairs and back to his car. I watch as he pumps a fist in the air before getting in as if celebrating a victory.

That true enthusiasm—reciprocated enthusiasm—is monumental.

It's another first for me.

Chapter Eleven

COOKIE

I THOUGHT I'd begun to understand what it means to truly care for someone with Stan, but now I realize I was only in it for what he could give me.

Being with Harris is completely different. Harris isn't just interested in sex or saving a damsel in distress to make-up for the fact that he couldn't save his sister. Harris isn't an in-your-face alpha male, though he has dominant qualities I appreciate.

As an alpha myself, I always thought it would be hard to find someone who could match my spirit, and still take the lead, as a man should do for his woman. After years of playing the submissive part, I know what I want in my own relationship. I just never thought I'd find a man who could give it to me.

Then came Harris. He appreciates my intelligence and independence. He's completely smitten and treats me like a real woman. He shows me he loves me in little ways. Like the time I washed my tennis shoes. I left them on the floor of my dorm for a few days because I couldn't be bothered with taking the time to re-lace them. One day, when I wasn't paying attention, Harris laced them for me and put them in my closet.

It sounds so silly, so simple, but those are the things I appreciate. I don't need Harris to buy me things. I don't want money or clothes or jewelry from him. I want exactly what he gives me: affection, time, and toe-curling orgasms.

After living in horrible conditions and being put in repulsive situations my entire life, sometimes I wonder what I did to deserve this amazing life. I've never felt happiness like I do walking on UNC's campus. And it's not just because Harris is often at my side.

It's the entire vibe. I was meant to be here. I was meant to get this education. I was meant to be something bigger.

All I can think of is that God put me through all those trails so I would appreciate this moment more than if I would have glided into it.

There are times when the reality of who I am and things I've done haunt me. I've lived a sordid life. I stole a man's money. What will happen if Harris finds out the truth about my past?

Every day gets better and better, and I get more comfortable in my new life. Days turn to weeks and the next thing I know; I've completed my first year of college. Looking back, I didn't think I would make it here at all, let alone get this far. But here I am, fulfilling my dream, and what makes it even better is Harris, who has been nothing short of amazing since we started dating.

If this is indeed a dream then I hope nobody wakes me up.

FALL

One of the first projects Professor Callahan announces for our Business 201 class is to create a fictional business and come up with the steps we need to get it running from the ground up. He gave us a rough outline of what to do, but we have to do the research about our particular idea.

I'm absolutely ecstatic. This is the kind of knowledge and experience most entrepreneurs don't get. Starting a business is a daunting task, especially to someone with no one to ask about it and zero start-up funds.

Then he says he's going to assign us a partner, so we get the added experience of having to compromise.

I'm not a group-work kind of person. I hate relying on other people to get things done and I especially hate that my grade comes down to work other people do. I'd rather have full control.

To make matters worse, I get paired with Charles Williams, the guy who wears a brightly colored Hawaiian shirt every single day and always seems light-years away. Is he a Magnum PI fan? Is he a surfer dude like Spicoli? Guess I'm about to find out.

When I arrive at the library, he's sitting at one of the front tables surrounded by paper and what looks like small, thin pieces of chalk.

"Hey, Charles!"

He looks up, brushes his sun-bleached hair out of his eyes, and gives me a huge smile. "Hey! Cookie! What's up?"

"I'm ready to get started on this project," I say, taking the seat across from him. I set my backpack in the chair next to me and I dig out a notebook and a pen. "Any thoughts about what kind of business we should open?"

"So, like, here's my idea," Charles begins looking at the ceiling as if he's reading it there. "For as long as I can remember, I've wished there was a place to get rad clothes without having to pay an arm and a leg. Trends change so fast these days. Some of us can't keep up."

I'm so excited to hear that someone thinks the same way I do, but I bite my tongue so I don't make a comment about trendy and his shirts.

Now that we're talking, I'm relieved to find that he's actually a smart kid. His head is in the clouds, but he's got some great ideas. And we have one huge idea in common.

"Yes! I've thought the same thing," I say, sitting upright in my seat. "Like those Swatch watches. They come out with new designs all the time. I can't even afford one, let alone multiple options."

"Exactly! Man, I thought this project was going to blow, but now I'm excited."

"Okay, so we've got our business. We've got to plan from the bottom up, right? See what we need to do to get it off the ground. Which means tons of research."

"Yep." He hunches over the table, getting back to work on whatever he was doing when I arrived.

I crane my neck to look get a better look. "What are you working on over there?"

"Just some designs ideas I had. They're for one of my art classes."

"You design clothing?"

He nods and shrugs at the same time. "Clothes, accessories, any crazy idea that pops into my head. I just draw what I see up here." He taps his temple.

"Charles! That's awesome! If you design the clothing, it saves us money on our bottom line because we won't have the cost of hiring a designer." I jot that in my notebook. "But how do we get them made? Have you researched that?"

"I've thought a lot about that, actually." He looks up from his sketchbook and sets his pencil down. "Broke college students will do anything to make some cash, right? I'm sure we can find people here that would do it. Or at a community college or something. I can design the clothes. My wife sews, but it's not possible for her to mass produce. She could make one set, and have the others copy her pattern. That way, we'd only need a few seamstresses. And we could pay a decent hourly wage."

"You really have thought about this, haven't you?" I ask, looking up from scribbling in my notebook, suddenly intrigued in ways that go far beyond a Business 201 project.

"Yeah." He rubs the back of his neck. "It's our dream to open a store. Nothing huge, just a small shop for regular people, like, the common man, ya know?"

A lightbulb goes on in my head. This could be a real business—not just a fictional one for a class.

"What's stopping you?" I ask, tucking one leg under my butt.

"What *isn't?*" he asks, with less enthusiasm in his voice. "Money is a huge issue. There are so many costs involved in starting a business, especially one with inventory needed for a store. Rent, utilities, employees, the cost of fabric, thread, zippers, sewing machines." He trails off defeated.

"I get it. The store and designs are just the tip of the iceberg. There's a lot more that goes into creating clothing than design and sewing."

He nods. "Exactly. Every time Jeni and I think about it we get discouraged. We'd definitely need a financial backer to start the project and we don't know anyone with that kind of cash who'd take a chance on a random store."

"Good thing we go to this school, eh?" I bump his arm with my elbow. "There are potential financial backers all over the place."

"Yeah, I know." He swallows and looks up sheepishly. "But it's not that easy to walk up to some rich kid and ask for money. As if they don't already look down on me."

My gut instinct is to tell him to suck it up and put aside his pride. A lot of people are born into shitty circumstances. The difference between those who succeed and those who don't is how they adjust and move forward. If you live as a victim, you'll always be one. If you take responsibility for your own life, you can change the course.

But I don't say any of that because I know my personality comes across as brash for some people. They rarely want to hear the truth.

Instead, I take the softer approach. "I get that, but if you have a dream you need to do what it takes to make it happen."

"And that's why I'm working three jobs while taking a full course load." He swipes his pencil off the desk and hunches over his sketch again. "I'll make it happen."

I nod, my head spinning with ideas.

With Harris' money and name, Charles' designs, and cheap seamstresses—we have a million-dollar idea.

Two years ago, I remember telling Stan I wished there were affordable clothing options. Things that looked trendy and high-end for a fraction of the price than what you can find at department stores. Talking to Charles about this project sparked an amazing idea. I'll have to talk to Harris about it, of course.

Over the last two years, he's has been trying to think of a way to stand out from his family. His older brother is being groomed to take over their property development company. The company is so big, there would definitely be a place for Harris, but he doesn't want to play second fiddle to his brother. He wants to shine on his own and prove he can bring value to the family rather than ride on their coattails.

If we could get a clothing store off the ground—and make it

successful—Harris would gain respect from his family for going a different way and making it work.

The designs are key. I'm not an artist, so I wouldn't be able to do that part, but we could always hire a designer. Harris knows everything that goes into running a business. If I could give him a comprehensive business plan, I'm pretty sure he'd go along with it.

For something that started as a random project for a business class, it's turning into an idea that could make Harris and I millions.

"What are you working on?" Charles asks, glancing at me quickly.

"I'm making a list of all the expenses so we can start researching. You know Professor Callahan will want a thorough project."

"Yeah. He won't accept half-assed anything." He straightens up. "Leave me a list of things you want me to research before we meet up next week. I'll get it done."

"I'm glad we got paired, Charles. Seems like we're a good match."

"Totally agree. This project's gonna be rad!"

Chapter Twelve

HARRIS

"Harris!"

I hear Cookie burst into the apartment before I see her. Hearing her voice and knowing she's mine still makes my heart skip a beat.

The moment I met Katrina at Mangione's, she enthralled and overwhelmed me. I wished I would have asked Beau for a way to contact her, but when she went off with Waylon, I dismissed the idea. When we re-met at registration, I knew it was fate, and I promised myself I wouldn't let her go again.

There's something about her that makes me want to be around her all the time. Not only because she's so grossly different from the women I grew up around; snobby kids who felt like anyone who wasn't in the same socioeconomic bracket was beneath them. But Cookie isn't like that, she has a down-to-earth appeal—and her smile. Oh God! Her smile could light up any room she walks into.

She's effortlessly beautiful—subtle, but impossible to ignore. And to crown it all, she's nothing short of brilliant. Some of my favorite moments were when I watched her in the Lit class we shared during the first semester of our Freshman year. She always had the answers and they were always correct—even if she had to debate to prove her point.

Watching her go head-to-head discussing Lady Macbeth with Professor Malcolm made all the blood rush to my dick.

"Harris, I have an amazing idea!"

"I'm in the kitchen, baby!" I call out, as I dice onions on the cutting board.

After our Freshman year, we decided to live together off-campus for our sophomore year. Over the summer, Cookie stayed in Chapel Hill and worked at a small jewelry shop while I went home to work construction. Being apart sucked so much, I came back every weekend to be with her.

Ever since we started living together, Cookie has made every meal. At first, it was a little rough, but she bought a cookbook and now the woman is like a Southern Julia Child. All she needed was some direction, something she said she never got from the aunt she lived with.

I planned on surprising her with a homemade spaghetti dinner tonight. But I got held up on campus and just started a few minutes ago.

"Pucker up, Harris, because you are going to want to kiss me after this!" She rushes into the kitchen holding a thick packet.

"I always want to kiss you," I say, leaning over and placing my lips on hers. She curls one hand in my hair, tugging gently.

"I feel the same way, Sugar," she whispers when we break apart. Her bottom lip glistens, which makes me want to grab it in my teeth.

"What's the big news?" I ask, resuming my chopping.

"You know how you've always said you want to do something other than work for the family business?" she asks.

I nod.

"I've got our opportunity right here." She slaps the front of the packet. "And I think it's going to be huge."

"I'm intrigued." I gesture for her to sit at the bar stool across from where I'm working.

She slides onto the chair and pulls her hair into a ponytail, securing it with a pink scrunchy thing she had around her wrist.

"Commons Department Store. Affordable fashion for the common man," she says with her arm outstretched as though she sees the words on a billboard.

I like the slogan. It's catchy, and it has the family name, but I'm not so sure about the idea. I hold my tongue before saying anything. Knowing Cookie, she has much more to share.

"A department store?" I ask.

"Yes!" she says confidently. "A department store for everyone selling affordable fashion. I've done the research." She opens the packet and flips a few pages. "I've even polled people in Charlotte, Chapel Hill, Raleigh, and Greensboro. There's a market for this."

"What's that?"

"It's a complete business plan."

"Really?" I set the knife down, sweep the onions into the pot on the stove, and wipe my hands on a towel. Then I take the booklet.

As I flip through the pages, I'm impressed at how thorough it is. From location to employees to projections—it has everything. My dick swells with each page I turn. Business plans get me off, but business plans made by the amazing woman in front of me take it to another level. There's nothing she can't do.

As I read through a few key pages, she goes into an explanation as if she's been waiting to tell me every detail for years. She's talking so fast, I think her head might start spinning.

"Did you come up with all of this?"

"Well, I had this idea years ago, but I didn't really start planning until last semester. It was a project for Business 201. My partner and I came up with it together."

My excitement dims slightly. I'd rather not go into any business with someone else—other than Cookie. "What about the partner? Does he—or she—want in on this business?"

Cookie shrugs. "I didn't ask. We came up with the plan together, but I did most of the research. Actually, I did *extensive* research. We used his clothing designs for the project."

"Are they in there?"

"What?" she asks, grabbing a cookie from the jar on the counter. I slap her hand playfully and set the packet down.

"Are the designs in the plan?" I rephrase my question, spinning around to get a jar of pasta sauce out of the cupboard.

She nods and reaches over, flipping to a page in the book that starts a series of design pages. "Well, we can't use these."

"True," she agrees, with a sparkle in her eye. "But we *can* have someone recreate them with slight differences."

"Your mind is so incredibly sexy."

"Just my mind?" she asks, slowly trailing her fingers from her neck to the collar of her yellow V-neck sweater.

My gaze slides to her chest. "I'm going to take you on this counter if you keep that up."

"Promise?" She winks. Then she gets up and rounds the counter to stand next to me. At first, I think she wants to get frisky, but when she looks at me, she's back to business. "Seriously though, what do you think?"

I twist off the cap of the sauce and dump it into the pot where I've been simmering onions. "The first step is calling Daddy to see what he thinks."

"Yeah?" Cookie hangs on my arm as she hangs on every word. Her eyes are wide and hopeful, like a child asking Santa for gifts.

I break into a grin. "I can't see him turning us down with all the work you've put into this." I flip through the pages quickly again. "It's got everything he would ask for."

Cookie beams as she looks at me. "Do you think we could make this work?"

"We're absolutely going to make this work."

I plan on making this woman my wife someday. I haven't said it, but we both know it—we both feel it. We were meant to be together, and nothing could tear us apart.

Chapter Thirteen

COOKIE

BEFORE THIS YEAR, if anyone ever asked me which was the best year of my life, I probably would have said the year I secured enough money to go to NCU and met Harris (again). But honestly, nothing could have prepared me for the avalanche of amazing things that happened this year.

Harris' parents approved the loan to help us start the department store and seemed genuinely excited about it. We'd hoped they would say yes, but we'd also prepared ourselves for an unfavorable conclusion.

Knowing they were enthusiastic about the store and willing to help in any way possible was a huge positive for us. In fact, I don't know if we could have pulled it off without their connections and assistance.

Spurred by excitement and drive to do this, neither of us wanted to wait until after graduation. We had an extensive plan, we had the funding, and we were determined to make it happen. But once we put the plan in motion it was a nonstop frenzy.

With help from many of the Commons family's contacts, we were able to get things going quickly. We secured a space in a popular strip mall off Park Road in Charlotte. As the store was being redesigned, we purchased fabrics in bulk at a huge discount from one of Mr. Commons' friends in the textile industry. We purchased sewing machines and used borrowed warehouse space to set up a place for our multiple teams of seamstresses to work on the clothing designs. We bought eclectic, affordable accessories from local artists as well as from overseas.

Harris worked on marketing while I acted as Project Manager, making sure we were on track and staying within budget. Despite having full class schedules at NCU, at least one of us—but usually both —spent almost every weekend in Charlotte. It was stressful, exhausting—and absolutely exhilarating.

With all the help we received from Commons friends and associates, we were able to open the store within six months from the date we signed our lease on the space. The best thing we did was hire two seasoned retail professionals to manage and run the store. They reported everything to Harris and I and told us if we needed to be there—outside of our weekend trips.

There are always a few hiccups when getting a business started. Thankfully, Harris' parents were able to help while we were in Chapel Hill. They've also been invaluable resources for efficiency ideas and troubleshooting. The entire experience gave me insight into a whole new world. A world where families support and motivate each other and having power and connections make things happen.

It's a world I've tied myself to. This business is half mine even if things with Harris and I don't work out. It seems callous to think like that, but I have to look out for my own best interests because there's no one to save me if this doesn't work out. I don't have a wealthy family to fall back on like he does and I'm never going back to Mama's ways.

NORMALLY, we would have gone to Charlotte this weekend, but I have a surprise for Harris, so I made sure we stayed in Chapel Hill.

"The Rolling Stones are in Raleigh right now and I don't have tickets. The Rolling Stones! Thirty minutes away," Harris moans, for the millionth time. If his face were any longer, his chin would hit the floor.

"It's okay, darling. You'll have plenty of other chances to see them," I say, trying to console him.

Part of me feels bad because The Rolling Stones really are Harris' favorite band and he's devastated he couldn't get tickets. Before we started dating, I could name a few of their songs—the really popular ones. But now I'm a mega-fan-by-default having heard all of their albums a thousand times.

The part of me that doesn't feel bad knows I have two tickets to the show at Carter Finley Stadium tonight in my purse. I bought them as soon as they went on sale and I've been keeping it a secret ever since. It's killed me because of how much agony Harris has been in.

"Um, Cookie, this is the *Rolling Stones.* They haven't toured in years because Mick and Keith were in some kind of feud," he explains. "Hell, with the life they've led, no one knows how long either of them will even be around."

I grab my purse and put a hand on the doorknob. "Are we still going to dinner or would you rather mope around all night?"

"Can we play Tattoo You in the car on the way to dinner?" he asks. The man is just pitiful.

"Absolutely, Sugar." I rub his back as he slides up next to me. He holds the door open so I can go out first. Always the gentleman even when he's upset.

When we get into his car, he cranks the engine and starts to back out. "Where do you want to eat?"

"There's this great place near NC State that I've been wanting to try," I say, rummaging in my pocketbook.

Harris breaks hard and turns to me. "You want to go to Raleigh for dinner? Cookie! I've got a nine a.m. class tomorrow!"

"I know, Sugar," I say, pulling the tickets out and holding them in front of him. "I thought we'd want to grab something close to the show."

Harris' eyes are popping out of his head. "Cookie, are those—" He plucks the tickets from my hand. "Oh my fucking God! You got us tickets to see the Rolling Stones!"

"Well, don't go takin' the Lord's name in vain now," I chastise.

"You—" He looks from the tickets to me. "—You are the most phenomenal woman on the planet!"

"I know." I wink at him.

After dinner at a cute little diner, we rush over to Carter Finley Stadium at North Carolina State University so we don't miss one moment of the action. The opening band is a new artist called Living Colour. Both Harris and I have only heard one of their songs, a hit called "The Cult of Personality," and we want to hear it live.

When it's time for the main act, Mick runs out in a long, green leather jacket with tails and the skinniest black jeans I've ever seen. I'm slightly jealous of how good his legs look in them.

When the band breaks into "Start Me Up," he entire crowd cheers and starts clapping in rhythm with the song. Harris puts his thumb and forefinger between his lips and whistles loudly.

He hugs me to his body as a thank you, then we both join the crowd bouncing and clapping. The entire concert has an electric feel. The crowd is buzzing. And Jagger has so much stage presence you can't help but enjoy the show.

I'd never been so proud than the day I skipped all my classes and waited in line—for hours—to get tickets for The Rolling Stones concert. I may have been beaming as I handed over *my* money—money I earned from our thriving business.

I've never had the means to spend money on something fun and frivolous before. It makes my heart happy to finally be able to buy such a significant gift for Harris. It's not a one-sided relationship when it comes to finances anymore. Maybe I couldn't contribute as much before, but now I can.

Harris and I are equals.

Chapter Fourteen

HARRIS

WHEN HEADLIGHTS FLASH through my bedroom window, I glance outside to see who's visiting.

"Not today," I groan when my brother jumps out of the car.

The store has been slammed and I didn't get home until after ten p.m. I'm so exhausted I could sleep for a week. The only thing I want to do right now is eat my supper in peace. I don't have the mental capacity to barb with Beau.

I disrobe quickly, tossing my dirty clothes in the hamper before heading downstairs to the dining room. My shower can wait. Let Beau smell me after an extra-long day in retail.

"What's happenin', hot stuff?" I ask, quoting Long Duk Dong from Sixteen Candles on my way down the stairs.

"You're lucky I'm in a good mood, asswipe," he says, reaching to slap my head as I blow by him. He misses, which earns him a burst of laughter from me.

"What's that smell?" he asks, following me into the dining room. "And why don't you have any clothes on?"

I smirk, but don't answer. Instead, I beeline to the kitchen to grab the plate Mama left in the refrigerator for me. When I remove the tin foil, there's a heaping portion of meatloaf, mashed potatoes, and collard greens.

"Mmmm mmmm! Mama loooooves me!" I sing as I pop it into the microwave and toss the foil in the trash. Then I grab a fork out of the drawer and wait for the time to tick down. The glorious scent wafting through the air makes my stomach growl.

Beau chuckles. "I do miss Mama's cooking."

"LuAnn doesn't have stove skills?"

"It's fine. It's just a variation of the same four meals every week. We order pizza every Friday," he replies. His voice is further away than I expect. When I glance over, he's inspecting the wine rack as if trying to decide what bottle to open.

"Aha!" he exclaims, pulling out a Concha Y Toro and examining the bottle like a prized trophy. "Cabernet Sauvignon," he mutters as he reads the label on the bottle.

I shake my head in amusement. Beau is the only person who can get away with touching Daddy's prized wine collection without asking.

"That's a lovely wine. Dry with a distinct cherry grip." My mouth waters just thinking about it. The alarm on the microwave goes off, and I grab my plate.

"Good Lord, you're a freak." He opens the top drawer of the buffet and removes a bottle opener. "A teenager with the taste buds of an old man."

"I'm twenty," I correct him, then wave my hand flippantly. "But never mind that."

He shakes the bottle in my direction as I slide into a chair at the dining room table. That thing better not slip from his hands and make a mess on the floor because I'm not in the mood to hear Mama wail about red wine stains on her carpet.

"Tonight, we celebrate, Harris!" he announces happily.

"What are we celebrating? My belated twentieth birthday?" I ask, before shoveling a scoop of mashed potatoes into my mouth.

He lifts the bottle to his lips and takes a taste. "This is the good stuff, brother," Beau concludes with a satisfied sigh.

"And yet, you drink like a savage, Captain." I shake my head. "Get two glasses from the kitchen cabinet. And grab the butter while you're over there, would ya?"

Beau moves to the cabinet and does what I ask—which surprises me.

"What's the news?" I ask which makes him smirk.

"Now you're interested." He rolls his eyes as he places the butter and two long-stemmed glasses on the table.

After slathering my potatoes, I push the container back toward him. "Take care of that."

He stops pouring and lifts his gaze to mine. "Do I need to beat your ass, brother?"

I snort and continue eating.

"You've finally proven your worth in our family," he announces after we've drained our glasses and refilled them. Beau's still grinning like a possum.

"That's pretty vague," I drawl, the alcohol already altering my mood at double the usual time. Commons Department Store has taken off, but Cookie and I haven't shared our numbers with anyone yet. So he can't be taking about that.

"That's some good shit," I mutter, glancing at the bottle on the counter.

"Remember when you were talking to Richard from King Electric?"

"Yup."

I shot the shit with the owner for an hour or so on a job site at the beginning of the summer when I went to say hi to the guys I used to work with. I'm too busy with the store to work on site anymore, but I do try to see the guys every once in a while.

"That conversation turned into some big talks between Daddy and Richard over the last few months. Old Man King must've taken a liking to you, because he called Daddy that very afternoon and discussed selling."

Interested, I stop eating and look up. "Selling what?"

"Selling King Electric to Daddy to be an offshoot of Commons Property Development. We'll have our own electricians. Cuts our costs and gives us more control."

"Are you kidding?"

"Would I have let you two knuckleheads share a bottle of my favorite Concha Y Toro if he were?" Daddy's voice booms from the doorway.

Beau and I both look up. I swallow hard and straighten in my seat. "Good evening, Sir."

"Looks like your brother told you the big news."

"It's amazing news," I agree. "Were you even looking for an electrical company?"

"No." Daddy strides into the room and lifts my wine glass. "But I've never been the kind of man who passes up an opportunity when presented with it." He takes a sip.

Truer words have never been spoken. Daddy is a risk taker and an opportunity grabber. His decisions and acquisitions took Commons from a small development company in North Carolina to multi-million-dollar corporation with projects across the South.

"King's been thinking of retiring, but didn't have anyone to take over his business. He said he got the idea to approach us after talking with you.

"The man even said that you might just take my place if I wasn't careful," he laughs. "The conversation got me thinking of my own retirement," Daddy says. "I want you and Beau to run the company together."

Beau opens his mouth without giving me a second to digest Daddy's statement. "Just think, Harris, with the two of us at the helm, Commons Property Development will dominate the market."

I take a deep breath, using the moment to contemplate the full-court press they've got going on. All my life, the only thing I ever wanted was to be as important as Beau—and to run Commons Property Development. They're offering me my dreams on a silver platter—with a glass of the finest Cab.

It finally dawns on me why Beau wants me on board so badly. I'm the idea man. I'm the hard worker. I'm the guy that makes things happen. And he's the guy who wines and dines clients.

"What do you say, son?" Daddy asks, smoothing down his Tom-

Selleck-wannabe mustache, seemingly uncomfortable by my lengthy silence.

My shoulders drop as I release a breath. "Thank you. I mean, I'm flattered and blown away by the offer, but—"

"But?" Beau asks, setting his glass on the table with a little more force than called for. "How is this even a question?"

Daddy doesn't speak, but his intense eyes narrow, waiting patiently for my answer.

"The store is blowing up," I reveal unable to keep the elation out of my voice. "Cookie and I plan on presenting the numbers to you soon, once we have something concrete drawn up, but revenue has exceeded our expectations."

"By how much?" Daddy asks.

"We were able to pay back your initial investment in the second quarter."

I've never seen my father dumbfounded, but that's the only word I can think of to explain his expression. But I'm not going to stop there because I really want to knock his socks off. "We're averaging thirty-five percent top-line growth and twenty percent profit growth per quarter."

"Are you kidding?" Beau asks. "Are those real numbers?"

I nod and lean back in my chair, gladly accepting my place as man of the moment. "I don't have the exact numbers on me right now, obviously. But I remember that much. It's been absolutely mind-boggling."

"I—well—that's"—Daddy stutters, searching for words.

I've never seen him speechless. I can't wait to tell Cookie.

I pour what's left of the bottle into my glass, then look up, remembering I should have offered it to someone else first. "I earned this, right?" I ask sheepishly.

"I'd say so." Daddy nods, his expression blank as if in a fog and trying to figure out how the conversation took such a twist. "I'll be honest, Harris. I didn't expect to hear that about the store. I'm pleased, don't get me wrong, but I'm surprised."

"You and me both, Sir."

"Guess we'll return to this subject at a later time. There's no hurry, since I'm not retiring anytime soon." He winks. "I'd like to see those numbers as soon as you have something ready for me."

I nod. "Absolutely, Sir. Cookie and I will work on it this weekend," I say as my father strides to the door.

I can't even look at Beau right now. I'm sure he's as surprised as he is disappointed. If the store continues this kind of growth and profit, I'll never work for Commons Property Development. I'll never be his puppet—making moves and taking the company to the next level in the background while he revels in the glory.

Daddy stops in the doorway and turns around. "I know we've had our differences about her in the past, but that Cookie really is quite a girl."

My jaw drops. After three years of arguing with my parents about my choice of girlfriend, I never thought I'd see the day my father would accept Cookie. But I know why.

It's because she proven her worth in his eyes. She may not be from one of Charlotte's elite families, but she's been instrumental in every single aspect of the store from conception to success. Hell, it was *her* idea.

I haven't kept her role in the shadows. Unlike Beau, I know the spotlight can be shared. If Commons Department Store becomes a household name, I want everyone to know my future wife helped me build the empire.

Katrina MacIntyre is the embodiment of a new, Southern woman. She has the intelligence and tenacity to hold her own in a board room with Daddy and any one of his peers.

And she makes one hell of a Pecan Pie.

Chapter Fifteen

COOKIE

"You should've been there, Sugar!" Harris exclaims after telling me the story of his trip to his parent's house this weekend. Unfortunately, I had to stay in Chapel Hill to finish up a group project.

We're lying in bed, wrapped in each other's arms after a round of passionate, sweaty sex. Harris is never rough and demanding. He likes to build up the tension with foreplay, then consume me until my toes curl and waves of powerful orgasms wash over me. He treats me like a treasure. Something to be handled with care. It's one of the many things that I love about him.

"I wish I would have been," I say, stroking his hair softly.

"Seeing both Beau and Daddy absolutely dumbfounded at our success was one of the best moments of my life."

His choice of words makes me smile. "*Our* success." Harris always makes sure he praises both of our efforts. It's such a relief to be with someone who does that without thinking.

Many men would take all the credit—especially in front of their older brother and father. Harris grew up with a powerful drive to prove himself, and has every reason to take the credit—yet, he didn't.

"You should have seen Beau, scowling at me, when I said I didn't want to be a part of the development company right now. It's like his lazy-ass finally realized he'll actually have to do work."

I laugh. "He'll be fine. If he's one of those guys who's always looking for a way to get ahead while doing the least amount of work possible, he'll find a way."

"True. He'll find another number two."

"You weren't put on this earth to be anyone's number two, Baby. You're a leader." I reach down to stroke his cock as I stroke his ego. "You have everything that you have ever wanted; your own successful business and your father's respect."

Harris moans at my touch and draws me closer. "I also have you," he whispers. "That's the biggest win."

With that, he pushes me up unto his chest with his hand grabbing my ass until our faces touch and we're kissing. In no time, he spreads me open with his fingers and slides inside me. The feeling is so intense, I can barely find the words to describe it.

Later that night, as I lie on Harris' chest, listening to his heartbeat, a million thoughts race through my head.

The success of the store caught all of us off guard—even Harris and I—our biggest cheerleaders. We knew there was a market for afford-able fashionable clothes and accessories, but we weren't prepared for the gusto in which how many people would jump on board with a new store with no name or brand recognition behind it.

We're about to open our second Charlotte location soon and have plans to for more if that one goes well.

I haven't heard from Stan since the day he left. It's like he vanished off the face of the earth. Though, his return is always in the back of my head, I don't let myself dwell on it.

He could be back in prison—or dead.

Or he could be on a flight to the United States right now.

I'm nervous because my entire life is a series of lies based on reality. I walk on eggshells, making sure I can recall every detail of this made up existence because I'm always on the cusp of everything blowing up in my face.

My last name isn't recognizable in banking or tobacco or one of the families who built the city. I'm not the daughter of one of Mrs.

Commons' sorority sisters or Mr. Commons' associates. While not quite arranged marriage, the wealthy definitely use a parental match-making system.

I'm actually impressed he hasn't succumbed to the pressure and ditched me for another girl.

Impressed, but not surprised. I know Harris loves me enough to fight for me.

If there's one thing I've taught myself is that worrying doesn't solve a problem, action does. If Harris and I are to be married and be together, I don't have a choice but to face his family.

No matter what happens.

Chapter Sixteen

COOKIE

MY HANDS SHAKE as Harris and I use a pair of obnoxiously over-sized scissors to cut the ribbon signifying the Grand Opening of the second Commons Department Store. When Rudson's, a chain out of Detroit, went bankrupt and had to close their location at Eastland Mall, we jumped at the opportunity to grab the prime location as an anchor store.

Never in a million lifetimes would I have thought I'd be the owner of a retail store with two locations before I even graduated college.

Yet here we are, smiles plastered on our faces as we shake hands and accept congratulations from the cream of the crop in Charlotte's business world. Harris keeps a hand on the small of my back, leading me through the crowd, stopping to chat with certain people and groups. He's a lifesaver. Being regarded in the high-powered business world has always been one of my goals—but it's still overwhelming.

I take a few seconds to enjoy the moment and reflect on how far I've come. Four short years ago, I was the poor girl from the wrong side of the tracks.

Today, I own a store in prestigious Eastland Mall. I helped create a business that has become so successful we were able to open a second location within two years of the first.

This weekend has been a bit of a whirlwind for me. Finals are coming up soon, so Harris and I have been studying as much as we can while still working our tails off. We've been in Charlotte for every school break and almost every weekend over the last year making sure the current store is running efficiently and everything for the new location was coming along properly.

Looking back on it, it probably would have made sense to take a year off school, but that wasn't an option—or even a thought—for either of us. We're both too driven to give up on something.

Despite all those trips, I never felt completely comfortable around Harris' parents until yesterday, when we got to town for the Grand Opening event. We weren't able to leave Chapel Hill until four in the afternoon because we both had Thursday classes. We got to his parent's house just in time for supper.

After a mild, yet intense, interrogation from the Commons' during dinner, it seemed as if I'd won them over. But as I helped Mrs. Commons clear the table and serve coffee, I heard commotion at the door. Harris' brother, Beau, and his wife, LuAnn, arrived for dessert.

At that moment, I thought the new life I'd worked so hard to build would blow up in my face. I'm positive Beau knows what I used to do, yet he's ever said anything—at least, not that I know of. It seems like a lifetime ago, but it's still raw. And I had no clue if he was going to mention it or not.

But nothing happened. Beau and LuAnn hugged me and said how pleased they were to finally meet me. Not one time during the conversation did it sound like someone who was holding something over on me or wanted to ruin me.

Maybe it's time to stop being so paranoid and start enjoying my life with Harris.

Chapter Seventeen

HARRIS

ON THE DRIVE TO CHARLOTTE, we've got the windows down and the music pumping. Cookie and I sing along to "Pour Some Sugar On Me" neither one of us missing a beat. I glance at her and smile, then place my hand on her thigh, inching up her short skirt the slightest bit so my palm touches her bare skin and my fingers come dangerously close to the promise zone.

Her breath gets heavy and she wiggles in her seat moving my fingers closer. I dip one finger into her panties thrilled with how soaked she is. She's always soaked for me like she can never get enough. She bites her lip and turns her head. I slide my fingers in and out.

The feel of her wet pussy against my fingers inflames my desire. If it were a little darker, I'd park on the side of the road and let her ride me until we both explode. She looks at me again, her eyes burning with lust. I remove my fingers and bring them to my mouth, loving how she tastes.

Luckily for me, I spot a motel down the road and I know this will be my only chance to satisfy my craving before we get to my family's house. Who knows if we will have the chance to have sex over the weekend?

"Sugar?" she says, employing the sultry tone I love.

"Yeah, baby?" I reply. We're getting closer to the motel and I just really want to fuck this woman.

"I want you, Harris. I want you now," she says, forcefully.

"I know, Baby, I want you too." I glance up at the road then smirk devilishly at her before speeding up and turning into the parking lot.

"See why I love you?" she asks playfully.

"Because we think alike," I answer, leaning forward to kiss her.

We scramble out of the car, and practically run to the entrance.

"Can I rent for the hour?" I ask the receptionist at the motel.

She looks up at me with a bored expression. "No."

"Oh, well, okay. Give us a room, please," I say, taking my wallet out of my back pocket.

The room is only twenty nine dollars for a night, and at this particular moment I can't think of a better way to spend thirty bucks.

About an hour and a half later, we're headed back to the car disheveled, but satisfied. The quickie—if you call fucking for an hour a quickie—was mind-blowing. When I open the door for Cookie, I notice her swollen lips match mine and her usually perfectly-styled hair is snarled and tangled.

"You're going to have to fix that," I tease, as she slides into the front seat.

"You, too! You can't walk into your parents' house with your hair sticking out all over," she retorts. It reminds me of how my hair got crazy—when she grabbed onto it while my face was between her legs.

We share mischievous looks and random laughs the rest of the way to Charlotte. One of my favorite things about Cookie is how refined she is, yet fun or kinky in the next breath. We literally just pulled off the road to have sex in a seedy motel. Then again, we've had sex in the car, on our balcony, even in my parents jacuzzi, so doing it in a motel shouldn't seem that crazy. We didn't even bother to take our clothes off because the short dress she had on made things easy.

I look at her now as she dozes, and can't help but smile. Cookie will probably kill me when she learns what I've got planned this weekend, but I'm not worried. Although we say those special three words often, they aren't enough to express how much I love this stubborn, sexy, intelligent woman. My life changed when I met her and I'm willing to do absolutely anything for her.

Every time we go to my parents' house, it's always the same. Everyone fusses over us. Cookie used to be overwhelmed by it, but she's gotten used to the attention. I'm just thankful my parents finally came around to her.

"I'm so excited," Mama mouths to me, before whisking Cookie away to the kitchen. Both of my parents know what's going on tonight. And they've been surprisingly chill since we got here. Normally, Mama can't keep her mouth shut when she has a secret.

"She's a smart one, your Katrina," Daddy says as we share a bottle of scotch in his study. If anyone else offered, I'd decline because I can't stand the taste of scotch. But I'd never turn Daddy down because that be plain disrespectful. "Reminds me of your mother when we were younger. It's no wonder why they get along so easily."

"I'm glad you like her, Daddy," I begin, looking into his eyes.

Age is beginning to show on Beau Commons Sr., but it does so with grace. It's also tempered some of his stubborn tendencies, so much so that it's still weird to hear him compliment Cookie after the fights we've had about her.

He sips his scotch, waiting for me to continue. He always knew when to listen and when to talk, a trait I inherited from him.

"As you know, I'm going to propose to her tonight after dinner. I need to be sure that you and mother will accept her," I say, putting my intentions on the table. This earns me a smirk and a chuckle from him.

"Knowing you, you would go ahead and marry her nonetheless and damn the consequences," he says.

I'm glad he understands that I didn't tell him because I'm seeking his approval. I've moved past that phase in my life.

"Of course, we'll accept Cookie. How could you even be worried? Your mother adores her. And with as long as you two have been dating, it's like she's already part of the family. I'm happy for you, son, and I'm damned proud of you," he says, hugging me. I'm pretty sure his eyes are shining with unshed tears, but my father would never let anyone see him be anything less than 'macho'.

"Speaking of children who make their father proud," I start as we break apart. "Where's the Captain?"

"He's in Europe at the moment," Daddy replies. "He said something about buying a soccer team in England or Spain." He takes another sip of his scotch. "For what it's worth, I believe it's going to be a profitable venture for him. Your brother's always been a big fan of soccer, right?"

"I believe it's called football over there, Daddy," I correct him but as expected he dismisses it.

"Bah! Potato, po-*tah*-to," he replies. "Oh, here they come." He motions to Mama and Cookie who can be seen from the large glass panel on the wall of his study. We put down our drinks and head out of the study to meet them.

It's showtime.

Chapter Eighteen

COOKIE

IF THERE IS one thing I've learned, it's that when you have a dirty past, life lures you into having a false sense of security. The feeling that everything is alright will always overpower whatever doubts you might have.

If his parents hadn't been present, I would've thought Harris was pulling a prank on me. I understand that he was bringing me to see his parents because it was a way to show how committed he is to me, but a proposal isn't something I expected.

Even the best actress on earth couldn't replicate my shock.

"Well, say something, Katrina," Mrs. Commons urges me, snapping me out of my reverie.

The woman is an absolute sweetheart, and I see where Harris gets his compassion and blue eyes. She's kind and warm and an amazing cook. I look forward to spending more time with her in the future and observing how to be a proper Southern woman. Lord knows I didn't get that from my own Mama.

While we were in the kitchen checking on dinner, she'd told me a little bit about herself. She wasn't born into a wealthy family, but she and Harris's father fell madly in love and he refused to back down, even when his father protested.

"You have nothing to fear, darling," she said as if she could tell that deep down, I'm not the rich girl I pretend to be.

"Katrina? Will you marry me?" Harris asks again. He's still on one knee, presenting me with the largest diamond I've ever seen. It's a solitaire on a simple gold band. Everyone's eyes are on me and the tension is palpable, maybe my silence set everyone on edge.

"Yes. Yes, of course, I will, Harris," I say, sounding breathless.

I'm elated and overwhelmed as Harris slides the ring onto my finger. As he pulls me into his arms, his parents clap and they come around to hug us.

My life is a true rags-to-riches story. Somehow, I have managed to escape a childhood, finish at the university, build my own business, and marry a rich man like Mama had always wanted.

If only she could me now. I think amidst the celebration.

Perhaps I should pay her a visit before we leave Charlotte to let her know I escaped my pitiful upbringing, and I did it without her help.

And that's where I made my mistake.

A FEW DAYS after our engagement, the Commons were on the front page of the Charlotte newspaper. Thankfully for me, I wasn't in any of the photos. I'm still not used to, or comfortable with, attention. Harris and I haven't taken engagement photos yet. Once we do, we'll be announced formally.

I fold the newspaper and set it on my lap, turning my gaze out the window. As the cab weaves through the familiar streets, I'm reminded of countless bus rides. This time, I have a pocketbook full of money that I earned on my own.

After the cab drops me off, I pay the driver, and make my way to the door with my head lowered, making sure that my face is mostly hidden. I'm not in the mood to be recognized.

When I knock on the door of my former apartment, a petite pretty Latino woman with doe eyes and an alert expression opens the door. I can't blame her for the paranoia, this neighborhood was never safe, and I see how much worse it's gotten.

"Hi there. I'm looking for my Miss. McIntyre," I say. "Is she available?" I look over her shoulder into the apartment.

She eyes me wearily and closes the door, so all I can see is her face. "She don't live here anymore. I move in a few months ago," she replies. "*Lo siento.*"

Damn," I mutter trying to think of where Mama could be. Could she have moved in with Aunt Polly after I left?

The woman must sense my distress because she continues, "I don't know if she's the same person but I hear that the last person was old lady who die of cancer," she says. "Neighbors say something about how she couldn't pay for treatment and her daughter was missing," she offers then begins to eye me warily.

"Oh. I'm sorry to hear that. It's actually her daughter that I'm looking for. We were close childhood friends." The lie rolls off my tongue but inside guilt rolls through me. "Thank you for your time. I'm sorry to have bothered you."

"*Buenas tardes,*" she calls as I shuffle down the hallway.

Once I'm outside, I lean against the door and take a deep breath.

I hated my mother. I hated what she put us through. I hated what she made me do.

I should feel sadness or guilt or regret, but I don't. I feel free.

I feel like today is the first day of the rest of my life.

Rolling my shoulders back, I smooth out my blouse and head back to the convenience store to use the pay phone. My head is down, watching my steps to make sure my heels don't get caught in a crack or on the uneven concrete.

When I glance up, I see a ghost—and it isn't my mother's.

Chapter Nineteen

COOKIE

"Get in the car." The Russian accent hits me like a concrete slab. I could ignore him and keep walking, but he's pointing a gun at me and it doesn't look like he's in a playful mood.

"Stan?" I whisper incredulously.

"Get in the car, Katrina. Don't waste my time," he says again, his voice sounding even edgier now so I oblige and climb into the sedan quietly.

"When I see the announcement of wedding. I think no. Cannot be my Katrina. But I know you will come to gloat to your mother, so I wait here every day waiting for you to show."

Every day? For how long? How long has he been in the United States? Why didn't he contact me?

"Your ego makes you predictable, Katrina," he snarls. "You stole my money." Stan accuses me.

"You told me to use it for what I needed," I fire back, barely able to contain the rage inside me.

He's the one who had to talk me into taking his stupid checkbook before he left. The gun pointed at me doesn't scare me at this point though, I have a feeling that Stan wouldn't hesitate to empty his bullets into me.

"There was over fifty thousand dollars in that account. What the hell could you possibly need for that much money?" he growls, his voice filling up space in the car.

"Living isn't cheap," I grumble. It's funny how we fall back into our old routine, almost as if he never left. The difference this time is that Stan isn't feeling very protective of me right now.

"But dying is," Stan replies coldly.

A shiver runs down my spine. This isn't the man I fell for. This is the mobster who killed a man in cold blood right in front of me. And I have no doubt he'd do the same to me without hesitation.

But my mother didn't raise a doormat.

"Are you threatening me?" I ask, my voice dangerously low to mask my fear.

He grabs my hair at the roots and yanks me forward until we're face to face, so close our breath starts to mingle. Once upon a time being so close to this man would make me stir with desire but now all I feel is disdain.

"Do you remember who I am? Do you remember what I could do to you?" he asks, his voice even deadlier now, but I feign calm.

"The tables have turned. *I* have the money, power, and a family name. *I* have control over you," I spit out, sounding more confident than I feel.

"Not if I kill you," he replies.

I lift my eyes to his, staring at him. "I have a feeling you'd rather fuck me."

"Does your pussy squirt hundred-dollar bills when I slide my cock inside?" Stan asks sarcastically.

"Maybe you should find out," I whisper, my voice hoarse with need.

His mouth crashes onto mine. I move my hands to his hair, pulling the roots as we kiss forcefully. When his tongue slides through my lips, I hold it and start sucking. He yanks my skirt up and pulls me onto his lap. Then he fumbles between us, pulling his pants down, and pushing my underwear aside.

In one hard thrust, he's inside me. I cry out, my head dropping to his neck. Using his shoulders for leverage, I ride him hard, grinding my clit on his pubic bone, taking his thick cock deeper and deeper. He bucks his hips, sending me sliding up and down.

We fuck—fast and hard and full of passion. I put all the anger, all the heartbreak, all the years of waiting—first in hope, then in fear —into it.

Once when he releases inside me, I know it's completely over.

"Is that what you wanted?" he asks, breathing heavily. He grabs the back of my hair and pulls my face away from his. "For me to take what's mine?"

"I'm not yours, Stan. I gave you the one thing I had to give any man. Giving you pussy is nothing special."

"You're the devil in disguise," he whispers, pulling up his black jeans and buttoning them quickly.

"*I'm* the devil?" I ask indignantly. "You murder people and *I'm* the devil."

"I've never murdered a man who didn't deserve to die." He shoves me onto the seat next to him before shifting the car into drive. "But you, Katrina, you preyed on me. You drew me in with your sob story and I fell for you."

"You knew exactly what it was. You called me out on what I was doing. And you left me your checkbook anyway. You left without leaving me with any way to contact you." I'm screaming now. Tired of his accusations. "For four years!"

"You had my money," he shouts each word back haltingly, his hazel eyes bulging out of their sockets.

"I didn't want your money. I wanted you!"

"You have four weeks to pay me back or I will kill you and your precious fiancé," he snarls. "Now get out of the fucking car."

Instead of waiting for me to do it, he leans over me, opens the door, and pushes me out.

As I tumble out of the car, my palms scrape against the cement while trying to brace my fall. My body shakes as I watch the car speed away from my position on my hands and knees. Rising slowly, I tug on the hem of my skirt with my fingertips, hoping I don't get blood on it. My heart pounds against my chest at how close I'd come to being killed.

I limp across the street to a gas station to wash up before calling a cab. Assessing the damage in the mirror, I shake my head. Other than swollen lips and messy hair, I don't look too rough from the neck up. But below is a different story. My hands are scuffed and bleeding, my blouse is a mess of wrinkles, my skirt is covered with streaks of dirt and multiple tears.

How am I going to return to the Commons looking like this?

How am I going to face Harris?

I've made bad decisions in my life. I've been ruthless and hard. But screwing Stan in a vulnerable moment shoots to the top of the list.

Chapter Twenty

COOKIE

FOUR WEEKS.

How am I going to come up with that kind of money in four weeks? I know we've made that much with the store, but I can't exactly tell Harris I need a check for fifty thousand dollars and not come back with a Cadillac or something extravagant.

When I get back to Harris' family's estate, I can barely look him in the eye. Thankfully, he is too busy going over numbers and plans with his father to notice my behavior is off.

It's a good thing I'm skilled at lying because the ride back to Chapel Hill would have been super awkward if I weren't. A three-hour car ride is much different than living with someone. I can't stay out of the apartment and I can't avoid him. We're far too intimate for him not to catch on.

Where am I going to get fifty thousand dollars in four weeks?

The pressure plagues me so much, I'm tempted to break down and ask Harris if I can take money out of the business account. We have it, but what am I going tell him I need such a large about for? Student loans? I already claimed to be a rich girl with enough money in her trust fund to pay for school.

Not surprisingly, it doesn't take long for him to catch on that something is off.

"Hey Cookie," he says one afternoon as we're making lunch together. "Can I ask you something?"

"Absolutely, Sugar." I lean over and kiss his cheek before grabbing a slice of salami from the package on the counter.

He lowers the knife he's been using to spread mustard on our sandwiches. "What's going on with you?"

My stomach drops, but I slap on a smile. "Whatever do you mean?"

"Something's been off recently. It's like you're trying to avoid me or not talk too much. You've been acting different ever since we got back from Charlotte." He places his hands on both sides of my face. "I'm worried about you."

I stare into his eyes and contemplate what to do. If I tell him the truth, I might lose the only man I've ever truly loved—and all the benefits that come with being with him. On the other hand, if I lie, I'll probably still lose him, and most likely die by Stan's hand, because I don't have the money to pay him back.

In the distance, the radio plays Bell Biv Devoe singing about a girl being poison, and the pressure of everything that's been weighing on me opens the dam.

Suddenly, I'm sobbing and explaining everything to him. The entire story of my life from how my mother pimped me out to my relationship with Stan.

Harris is quiet throughout my narration, but he doesn't release me from his hold, which I hope is a positive sign.

"You probably don't even want to marry me after all that. I wouldn't blame you," I say between sobs. At first, he doesn't answer, just stares over my head into space. "Harris? Please look at me," I plead.

"How long were you with him?" he asks, slowly bringing his focus to me.

"Two weeks," I confess.

"Did you love him?"

"No, but he made me feel cared for. He made me feel secure. I'd never had that before." Tension builds inside me because questions like this never bode well for the person being interrogated. But I refuse to lie again.

"How long have we been together?" he asks.

"Four years," I say, my voice low now.

This is the end, I think, already resigning to my fate.

"Would you rather be married to mafia scum?" Harris asks.

"No! I love you," I whisper, swallowing hard and grabbing the collar of his shirt in desperation. "Only you."

"Then I think you know my answer," he says. A smile creeps onto his face, but I feel like I'm imagining it.

"You don't think I'm trash after finding out about my past?" I ask, confused about his reaction. It isn't what I'd been bracing myself for.

"No. I don't think you're trash. I knew something was off, Cookie. You claimed to have an inheritance from wealthy parents in Charlotte. But if that were true, we would have known each other. We would have run in the same circles or heard each other's names. And—" Harris trails off.

"You had me researched," I whisper, as the realization suddenly hits me. I should've considered that already. Wealthy people like the Commons would have investigated my background.

"My parents did. About a year after we started dating," he corrects me.

"And they let you stay with me? Seems highly unlikely especially with all the affluent women here." I gasp, thinking of what his mother had said to me on the evening we got engaged.

"You have nothing to fear," she'd said. She knew my background and didn't treat me like I was scum. The thought brings tears to my eyes.

"I won't lie to you, Sugar. We had a few arguments about you." He chuckles.

"What tipped the scale to my side?" I ask, still not believing my ears. I have to be the luckiest woman alive.

"I think you're an amazing, strong, powerful woman. I can't believe you lived through being raised like you did and came out as amazing as you are. You're a fighter. You'll do what you have to do to succeed."

Hearing how he thinks of me brings me to tears. How do I deserve this kind of love? After my life. My mistakes. My lies.

He wipes my eyes with his thumbs. "And you are one hell of a business woman, Cookie. You're smart, determined, and persistent. I want you by my side for the rest of my life."

"I love you so much, Harris. Thank you for seeing me for the woman I am, and not holding my past against me." I wrap my arms around him and bury my face in his chest. He squeezes me to him.

"I love you too, Sugar. Can you promise me one thing?" he asks. I lift my head. "Promise that you'll always tell me what's going on. There's nothing we can't get through together."

I nod.

"So, we owe this Stan character fifty thousand dollars, correct?" Harris asks.

The pronoun he uses doesn't escape my notice. He isn't treating this as a mess I caused, instead he's taking it on like it's a joint problem.

My love for this man intensifies. He embraced me when most men would have tossed me out of their houses like a mangy dog.

"When we're in Charlotte this weekend, we'll get everything squared away, okay?" he asks after a moment of silence.

I nod. In my head, I say a silent prayer that I found Harris Commons.

Chapter Twenty-One

COOKIE

STAN AGREED to meet us in the same place I met him four years ago—
the alley next to the building he planned on buying. The building
hasn't changed, except maybe to deteriorate even more.

As a precaution, Harris hired a security team to accompany us just
in case Stan got any crazy ideas. Not that a security team would help if
he decides to pull out a gun and go Mafia hitman on us, but it makes us
feel better to have them there.

Mind over matter.

I have to hand it to Harris, he looks menacing as he faces Stan. Not
in the scary, feral way the Russian does. Harris has the refined, calm
demeanor of someone with power and money. He doesn't need
weapons to ruin someone's life. He could make a few calls, and end
Stan's life in a heartbeat if he threatens me again.

"Let's make this short and sweet, okay, Rybakov?" Harris begins, his
voice calm but with a definite edge to it. "I understand that you loaned
my fiancé some money to get through her university education. Cookie
and I are both here to personally thank you for your generosity."

"Loaned?" Stan laughs. "She—"

Harris raises his hand to silence the man who towers over both of
us. Surprisingly, Stan obliges. His eyebrows narrow at Harris, as if

wondering who the hell he is and what authority he has. My pulse races because Stan isn't the kind of person to submit. Maybe I don't understand levels of power.

"This is seventy thousand dollars," Harris says, pulling out a fat envelope filled with hundred-dollar bills. "The fifty we owe you and twenty for interest over the last four years."

Stan snatches the envelope out of Harris' hand as if he thinks he'll take it back.

"Stan, I—" I pause, trying to gather my thoughts. "I just want you to know that I didn't mean to screw you over. I, just," I swallow hard and blink back tears. "You know I needed to get out of here. You wanted that for me, remember?"

He stares at me with no expression, just blank eyes and straight, grim lips. He's standing so still, it's almost as if he isn't even breathing.

I continue because I owe it to him. I owe him this and much more. "I knew that I could make something of myself if I had the opportunity. I always planned to pay you back." I open my pocketbook and rummage for the envelope I have for him.

"This is the deed for this building. We acquired it in your name." I shove the envelope at him.

Stan's expression finally changes. First, he looks stunned, then curious. "This is some trick?" he asks, as his gaze shuffles between Harris and I.

"It's no trick," I assure him.

"It's no trick, but there *is* a stipulation," Harris says.

"Fuck your stipulations."

Harris continues undeterred, "I know everything about you, Stanislav. I know who you work for and I know who wants you dead. One phone call is all it would take and you'd be out of our lives forever."

Stan scowls, but raises an eyebrow and keeps listening. I never thought Mafia were patient, but I'm seeing a whole new side of life. Everything is about deals.

"You will never contact me or my family. You won't even come close to us. We don't run in the same circles, so this shouldn't be a problem, right?"

Stan grunts.

"If you do, I will ruin you," Harris says. He's so calm and collected, it's like he does this every day. "Understood, *Slava?*"

"*Da*. Understood." Stan nods in assent.

My heart speeds up, enthralled with Harris' remarkable display of power. He had the upper hand the entire time and didn't show any signs of intimidation.

"We're done here," Harris announces. "You ready, Sugar?"

He slides an arm across my shoulders, pulling me close as we walk back to the car together.

I owe Stan my life. But I repaid my debt and I need to move forward. Making amends and walking away from him means leaving behind my dark past and moving toward a bright future.

Usually, I feel safe in Harris' arms, but I make the mistake of turning back one last time.

There's darkness in the menacing smirk that slides across the mobster's face. My heart races causing an involuntary shiver at the unspoken message.

This isn't over.

EPILOGUE

COOKIE

I STARE AT THE WHITE, plastic stick.

Two blue lines.

My gaze flashes to the second stick. Then the third.

I thought the first might have been a false positive, so I grabbed a two-pack while I was at the pharmacy. It's always better to be sure.

Two blue lines.

I'm sitting on the toilet, holding my head in my hands. My knees shake as I try to figure out the moment of conception. My head swirls as I count backward.

"You almost ready?" Harris asks, entering the bathroom.

Normally, I wouldn't mind him coming in, but today, I spring to my feet with my arms extended, as if to push him out. "Harris, I, wait—"

When he spots the sticks on the sink, his expression goes blank. He looks up at me, then down at the sticks, then back up at me.

"Cookie?" he asks.

"I'm pregnant," I confirm with a small smile.

Instantly, his face lights up with elation and he pulls me into his arms. "We're pregnant? We're having a baby?" He backs away to check my face.

I nod.

"Must've been that quickie on the way to Charlotte, eh?" He wiggles his eyebrows.

Outside, I laugh softly and nod. Inside, I'm reeling because I know what scenario is more likely.

Harris is always careful. He insists on wearing a condom, even after we got engaged. As old school as it sounds, he'd be shunned by his family if we had a child before marriage. Even during our quickie, he was covered.

But I didn't use any protection during that anger-filled, passionate encounter with Stan.

I close my eyes, and snuggle into Harris' arms, praying my calculations are wrong.

If they aren't, I can only hope that no one will notice if the baby doesn't have any of my fiancé's features.

THE END

In a world filled with death and danger, my salvation comes in the form of one ruthless mobster ... who sets my blood on fire.

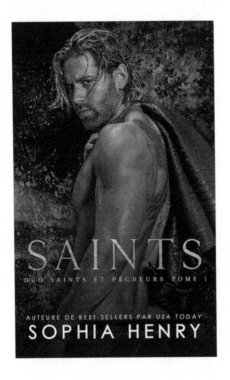

When my twin brother defects from Moscow to play hockey in America, a merciless gang sets their sights on me as part of an extortion plot.

The leader of a rival operation offers to keep me safe...for a price. In exchange for their protection, he wants my body. And as badly as I want to say no, body over life seems like a better deal.

But as I slip deeper into his world, the rival gang's leader demands more from me. Now he wants the only thing I'm unwilling to give him.

My heart.

If you like blazing-hot chemistry, a heart-racing plot, and gut-wrenching emotion then you'll love Sophia Henry's gripping Saints & Sinners duet.

**Turn the page to start reading
SAINTS now!!**

SAINTS EXCERPT

DMITRI MOROZOV IS DEAD TO ME.

Considering our history, it should be an easy decision to make, but today's interaction sealed my hatred.

When I reach the Metro, I rush down the stairs with tears still streaming down my face. The platform is so congested, I have to elbow my way through the doors. There will be another one in a few minutes, but it's Friday night and waiting won't make a difference. Either way, I'll be fighting the crowd; the people wearing drab, gray work clothes, on their way home for the day, or those with slight pops of color, dressed up to go out for the evening.

Maybe that's what *I* should do. When I get home, I should get dressed up, call Svetlana, and ask her to meet me at the discotheque. Maybe letting loose to Victor Tsoi's latest song is just what I need to help me drown away the pain of Dima's cold indifference when I asked him if he knew about my brother's defection to America.

The train jolts abruptly before heaving forward as it leaves the station. I plant my feet firmly for balance and tighten my grip on the bar overhead.

I haven't stopped crying since I left the Central Scarlet Army's hockey training base. Thankfully, anyone who's glanced my way has quickly averted their gaze. I close my eyes and take a deep breath, wiping away tears with the back of my free hand.

All I wanted was some answers. My twin brother, Vanya, who has shared everything with me since the womb, defected to the United States after a tournament in Sweden. Despite us being so close, he never uttered one word about it before he left. I thought going to Dima, his best friend on the team, would help me understand how my brother could have kept such a huge secret from me.

But the arrogant coward refused to reveal what he knew.

They were roommates. Friends! Was he not concerned or—at the very least—*inquisitive* when Vanya packed his bags and left?

Dima said he's scared. *He's* scared.

My family is being treated like criminals—being followed and questioned by the KGB—because of Vanya's desertion, and *Dima* is scared.

To be afraid is normal, but when a lieutenant in the military is a coward? That's unacceptable. Those in a position of power who have the ability to help must rise up. Though there may have been a time when I had feelings for him, I have no use for a chicken like him in my life.

When the train stops at *Aviamotornaya* station, I feel so numb and disoriented, it's as if the crowd is carrying me out the doors and up the stairs. I've walked home from here so many times, I do it on autopilot.

Vanya used to scold me for walking alone because the streets have gotten colder and darker over the last few years. He wasn't concerned about the weather or season, but the criminals and the violence they bring.

Mafia is everywhere, but I'm not scared. Gangs kill for money, power, and greed. They want something that someone else has.

I have nothing.

Besides, the *Bratva* is the least of my concerns. I have more to fear right in my own home. Ever since Mama died, I've become the lone target of my father's anger and violence.

Vanya's hockey accomplishments were the only bright moments in our mundane conversations. Now, we have nothing—just the bleak reality that he left us all behind.

For years, my brother swore he'd take me with him if he ever got the chance to live in America. He promised me again just a few weeks ago, minutes before he left for his most recent hockey tournament.

And now he's gone. And I'm here, stuck amid chaos and instability unlike anything I've ever lived through before in Russia.

At least life under communism was stable—boring, but stable.

The KGB has already harassed Papa, *Babushka*, and half of the other families who live in our apartment, asking them what they knew about Vanya's defection. It's only a matter of time before they come for me.

The thought of a KGB interrogation makes my stomach lurch. Though I rarely drink, I may join my father at the table with a glass of vodka tonight. I need something to numb the anger, betrayal, and heartbreak stewing for Vanya.

The concentrated gasoline smell permeates the air. I've gotten so used to the influx of vehicles taking to the roads over the last few years, I don't usually notice. But today, anxiety has my sensitive stomach bubbling with every inhale.

I've just crossed *Aviamotornaya Ulitsa* when, out of the corner of my eye, I notice a rusty Vaz creeping up the street. My jaw twitches involuntarily. Feeling a bit stupid for being nervous of an old car, I nuzzle my chin into my scarf and keep my gaze forward until it passes.

The loud rev of an engine makes me jump, and a shiny, black sedan speeds past and screeches to a stop a few meters ahead of me. My legs shake and I stumble over an uneven crack in the sidewalk.

Vaz is a common brand here, but black BMWs are only driven by mafia. Being stuck in the middle of crossfire between two gangs was not how I expected the day to end. But it's also not a surprise considering how the rest of it has gone.

I hold my breath, watching intensely as the sedan's driver and passenger doors fling open at the same time. Two men covered in black head-to-toe jump out and sprint toward me. My heart thumps in beat with their heavy footsteps pounding the concrete, each step getting louder as they get closer.

Swallowing back fear, I increase my speed and move to the side, giving the men space to get wherever they're going.

Suddenly, the taller of the two clasps his thick arms around me and starts carrying me toward the car. The other crouches down, grabs the bag I dropped, and sprints to the driver's side.

"No!" I scream as I kick my feet and fight to free myself. "Stop!"

It's a futile effort. There's no one on the road other than the Vaz, and the people inside know better than to try to stop mafia.

I stretch my legs to the ground, dragging my feet in an attempt to slow him down, but instead of having any effect, my shoes scrape against the sidewalk and one falls off. He tightens his grip and lifts me into the air.

When we get to the car, he yanks the door open and shoves me in face-first before slamming the door shut. It jars my feet, propelling my body forward and sending my cheek sliding across the seat.

"Please!" I cry out. "Please don't do this!" My clammy palms slip on the leather as I try to claw myself upright.

Instead of responding, the passenger spins around and leans forward. Cold sweat beads on my forehead as I scramble backward, pressing my spine against the seat. He wedges himself between the two front seats, grabs a fistful of hair, and pulls me toward him. I shake my head violently, but his grip doesn't loosen, and my jerky movements only enhance the pain.

He deftly wraps rope around my wrists, pulling it tight before making a complicated knot. When he's finished, he looks up. Icy blue eyes peer at me through the opening of the black balaclava masking his face.

When I gasp, he slams a foul-smelling rag against my mouth and I involuntarily ingest whatever's on the cloth. Only one thought runs through my head before everything goes black.

I know those eyes.

DON'T MISS OUT!

Get ALL the Sophia Henry news!

Sophia Henry's mailing list is the place to be if you like steamy romance novels that tug at your heart strings. Stay notified of new releases, sales, exclusive content with newsletters twice a month. Get a FREE book when you sign up at sophiahenry.com.

JOIN SOPHIA'S READER GROUP

When you join Sophia's Patreon Community you get exclusive access to AUDIO of her books, get sneak peeks, exclusive posts, and extra surprises just for members. You even get to name characters! (Seriously, it happens. Sophia's readers named Zayne, the hero of CRAZY FOR YOU).

Join the Fun: patreon.com/sophiahenry313

MERCH STORE

THANK YOU so much for taking the time to read DEVIL IN DISGUISE. I truly appreciate every single one of you. If you enjoyed reading DEVIL IN DISGUISE as much as I enjoyed writing it, it would mean the world to me if you would consider leaving a review on Amazon.

(If you really loved the book, copy and paste the same review to Bookbub & Goodreads!)

x Sophia

PLAYLIST

Complete Playlist on YouTube : SophiaHenryOfficial

Here With Me - Marshmello (feat. Chvrches)
Stubborn Love - The Lumineers
Hold Me Down - Halsey
Hallelujah - Panic! At The Disco
Underdog - Alicia Keys
I See Red - Everybody Loves An Outlaw
Wish I Never Met You - Loote
Break Me - The Band Camino
Señorita - Shawn Mendes
Shape of You - Ed Sheeran
Renegades of Funk - Rage Against The Machine
Better Now - Post Malone
D'yer Mak'er - Led Zeppelin
Never Tear Us Apart - INXS
Let You Down - NF
Don't take the Money - Bleachers
Ohio - Andrew McMahon in the Wilderness
Surrender - Walk the Moon
All My Life - K-Ci & JoJo
Greek Tragedy - The Wombats

ALSO BY SOPHIA HENRY

SAINTS AND SINNERS SERIES

Ebook and Paperback Available on Amazon

SAINTS

SINNERS

AVIATORS HOCKEY SERIES

Ebook and Paperback Available on Amazon

DELAYED PENALTY

POWER PLAY

UNSPORTSMANLIKE CONDUCT

JINGLE BALL BENDER: An Aviators Hockey Short Story

BLUE LINES

STANDALONE CROSSOVER NOVELS

EVEN STRENGTH

Saints & Sinners/Aviators Hockey Crossover Novel

DEVIL IN DISGUISE

Material Girls/Saints & Sinners Crossover Novel

MATERIAL GIRLS SERIES

Ebook and Paperback Available on Amazon

OPEN YOUR HEART

LIVE TO TELL

CRAZY FOR YOU

FOREIGN EDITIONS

FRENCH

SAGA MATERIAL GIRLS

OPEN YOUR HEART

LIVE TO TELL

CRAZY FOR YOU

DEVIL IN DISGUISE

DUO SAINTS AND SINNERS

SAINTS

SINNERS

ROMANS AUTONOMES LIÉS AUX SAGAS

EVEN STRENGTH

Saints & Sinners/Aviators Hockey Crossover Novel

SAGA AVIATORS HOCKEY

JINGLE BALL BENDER

BLUE LINES

GERMAN

MATERIAL GIRLS SERIES

OPEN YOUR HEART

LIVE TO TELL

CRAZY FOR YOU

RUSSIAN

SAINTS AND SINNERS SERIES

SAINTS

SINNERS

ABOUT THE AUTHOR

USA Today Bestselling Author Sophia Henry is a proud Detroit native who fell in love with reading, writing, and hockey all before she became a teenager. After graduating with a Creative Writing degree from Central Michigan University, she moved to warm and sunny North Carolina where she spent twenty glorious years before heading back to her roots and settling in Michigan.

She spends her days writing steamy, heartfelt contemporary romance and posting personal stories in her Patreon community hoping they resonate with and encourage others. When Sophia's not writing, she's hanging out with her two high-energy sons, an equally high-energy Plott Hound, and two cats who want nothing to do with any of them. She can also be found watching her beloved Detroit Red Wings and rocking out at as many concerts as she can possibly attend.

Receive a FREE ebook and get all the latest releases and updates exclusively for readers! Subscribe to Sophia's newsletter today.
https://bit.ly/FreeSHBookNL

Made in the USA
Columbia, SC
26 January 2023

10236374R10081